SCANDAL:
UNCLAIMED
LOVE-CHILD

SCANDAL: UNCLAIMED LOVE-CHILD

BY

MELANIE MILBURNE

First published in Great Britain 2010
Large Print edition 2011
Harlequin Mills & Boon Limited,
Eton House, 18-24 Paradise Road,
Richmond, Surrey TW9 1SR

ISBN: 978 0 263 22171 8

Harlequin Mills & Boon policy is to use papers that are
natural, renewable and recyclable products and made
from wood grown in sustainable forests. The logging and
manufacturing process conform to the legal environmental
regulations of the country of origin.

Printed and bound in Great Britain
by CPI Antony Rowe, Chippenham, Wiltshire

To Carey and Laura Denholm,
such wonderful friends and fabulous company. Thanks
for being there for us when we needed it most and
thanks too for all the side-splitting jokes! XX

CHAPTER ONE

BRONTE was doing a hamstring stretch at the barre when she heard the studio door open. She looked in the wall-to-ceiling mirror, her heart screeching to a halt when she saw a tall dark figure come in behind her. Her eyes flared in shock, her hands instantly dampening where they clung to the barre. Her heart started up again, but this time with a staccato beat which seemed to mimic the frantic jumble of her thoughts.

It couldn't be.

She must be imagining it.

Of course she was imagining it!

It couldn't be Luca.

Her mind was playing tricks. It always did when she was tired or stressed. And she was both.

She curled her fingers around the barre,

opening and closing her eyes to clear her head. She opened them again and her heart gave another almighty stumble.

It just couldn't possibly be Luca Sabbatini. There were hundreds, no, possibly thousands of stunningly handsome dark-haired men who might just by chance wander into her studio and—

'Hello, Bronte.'

Oh, dear God, it was him.

Bronte took a slow deep breath and straightened her shoulders as she turned and faced him. 'Luca,' she said with cool politeness. 'I hope you're not thinking of booking in for the first class of the afternoon. It's full.'

His dark eyes roamed over her close-fitting dance wear–clad body slowly, lingering for a heart-stopping moment on her mouth, before meshing his gaze with hers. 'You look as beautiful and as graceful as ever,' he said as if she hadn't spoken.

Bronte felt a frisson of emotion rush through her at the sound of his voice: rich and dark and deep and smoky with its unmistakable and beautifully cultured Italian accent. He looked the same as the last time she had seen him, although perhaps a little leaner if anything. Well over six feet tall, with glossy black hair that was neither short nor long, neither straight nor curly, and with the darkest brown eyes she had ever seen, he towered over her five feet seven, making her feel as dainty and tiny as a ballerina on a child's music box.

'You've got rather a cheek to come here,' she said with a flash of her gaze. 'I thought you said all that needed to be said two years ago in London.'

Behind his eyes it looked as if a small light had gone on and off like a pen-sized flashlight. It was a tiny movement and she would not have seen it at all if she hadn't been glaring at him so heatedly. 'I am here on business,' he said, his voice sounding a little rusty. 'I thought it might be a good chance to meet up again.'

'Meet up and do what exactly?' she asked with a lift of her chin. 'Talk about old times? Forget about it, Luca. Time and distance has done the trick. I am finally over you.'

She turned and walked back to the barre. 'I have a class starting in five minutes,' she addressed him in the mirror. 'Unless you want to be surrounded by twenty little girls in tights and leotards, I suggest you leave.'

'Why are you teaching instead of dancing?' he asked as his gaze held hers steady in the mirror.

Bronte rolled her eyes impatiently and turned back to face him. She placed one hand on her hip, her top lip going up in a what-would-you-care curl. 'I was unable to make the audition at the last minute, that's why.'

A small frown pulled at his brow. 'Were you injured?'

Bronte suppressed an embittered smile. Heartbroken and pregnant sort of qualified for injury, didn't it? 'You could say that,' she said, sending him a cutting look. 'Teaching was the next best option. Back home in Melbourne seemed the best place to set up to do it.'

His dark gaze swept over the old warehouse Bronte and her business partner Rachel Brougham had fashioned into a dance studio.

'How much rent do you pay on this place?' he asked.

A feather of suspicion started to dust its way up Bronte's spine. 'Why do you ask?'

One of his broad shoulders rose and fell in a non-committal shrug. 'It's a sound investment opportunity,' he said. 'I'm always in the market for good commercial property.'

She frowned as she studied his inscrutable expression. 'I thought you worked in hotel management for your family?'

Luca smiled a ghost of a smile. 'I've diversified quite a bit since I saw you last. I have several other interests now. Commercial property is a sure bet; it often gives much better returns than the domestic property market.'

Bronte pressed her lips together as she worked on controlling her emotions. Seeing him like this, unannounced and unexpected, had thrown her completely. It was so hard to maintain a cool unaffected pose when inside she felt as if she had been scraped raw. 'I am sure if you contact the landlords they will tell you the place is not for sale,' she said after a short pause.

'I have contacted them.'

She felt her spine slowly turn to ice as her eyes climbed all the way back up to his. 'A…and?'

His half-smile gave him a rakish look. It was one of the things that had jump-started her heart the first time she had met him in a bookshop in London. Her heart was doing a similar thing now, for all her brave talk of having got over him.

'I have made them an offer,' he said. 'That's one of the reasons I am here in Australia. The Sabbatini Hotel Corporation is expanding more and more globally. We have plans to build a luxury hotel in Melbourne and Sydney and another on the Gold Coast of Queensland. Perhaps you have heard about it in the newspapers.'

Bronte wondered how she could have missed it. In spite of her animosity towards him, from time to time she couldn't stop herself trawling the papers and gossip magazines for a mention of him or his family. Only a few months ago she had heard of the separation of his older brother Giorgio and his wife Maya. She had also heard something about his younger brother Nicoló winning an obscene amount of money playing poker in a Las Vegas casino. But she had heard nothing of Luca. It was as if for the last two years he had completely disappeared off the news media radar.

'No, but then again I have better things to do with my time,' she said with a disparaging look.

His dark eyes continued to hold hers in a stare-down Bronte was determined to win. She tried to keep her expression masked but even so his presence was having an intense effect on her. She could feel her skin tightening all over, her heart was racing again and her stomach was fluttering with a frenzied flock of razor-sharp wings. Seeing him again was something she had never allowed herself to think about. On a cold, miserable, grey day in November almost two years ago he had brought their six-month affair to an abrupt and bitter end. Her love for him had over time cooled down until it was now like a chunk of sharp-edged ice stuck right in the middle of her chest. What sort of naïve fool had she been to have loved such a heartless man? He had not once returned any of her calls or emails. In fact she suspected he had switched addresses and numbers in order to get her out of his life.

And now he was back as if nothing had happened.

'Why are you here?' she asked with a pointed glare. 'Why are you *really* here?'

He continued to look down at her from his towering height, but something about his expression had softened slightly. His dark eyes reminded her of melted chocolate, his mouth a temptation equally irresistible. She could almost feel those sculptured lips pressing down on hers. Her lips tingled with the memory and, as she thought of how he had made her feel in his arms, her chest felt as if someone was slowly pulling scratchy pieces of string from all four chambers of her heart.

Bronte felt her guard lowering and hastily pulled up the drawbridge on her emotions, standing stiffly before him, her arms folded across her middle, her mouth tight with renewed resolve.

'I wanted to see you again, Bronte,' he said. 'I wanted to make sure you are all right.'

She blew out a breath of disgust. 'All right? Why wouldn't I be all right?' she asked. 'Your ego must be far bigger than I realised if you think I would be still pining over you after all this time. It's been nearly two years, Luca. Twenty-two months and fourteen days, to be exact. I've well and truly moved on with my life.'

'Are you seeing anyone?' he asked, still watching her in that rock-steady hawk-like way of his.

Bronte pushed up her chin. 'Yes, as a matter of fact I am.'

He gave no outward sign of the news affecting him but she sensed an inner tension in him that hadn't been there before. 'Would your current partner mind if I stole you for dinner this evening?' he asked.

'I am not going out with you, Luca,' she said with deliberate firmness. 'Not tonight, not tomorrow night, not ever.'

He moved a step closer, his hand coming down

on one of her arms to stop her from moving away from him. Bronte looked down at his long, dark, tanned fingers on her creamy bare skin within touching distance of her breasts, and felt her body shiver all over. It felt as if her blood was being heated to boiling point from that simple touch. She felt the drum roll of her heart and the deep quiver of her belly as his fingers subtly tightened. 'Is one night so very much to ask?' he said.

She pushed at his hand but he brought his other one over the top and held her firm. He was too close. She could feel his warm minty breath on her face. She could smell his lemon-based aftershave. She could feel her body responding as if on autopilot. 'Don't do this, Luca,' she said in a cracked whisper.

'Don't do what?' he asked, holding her gaze steady with his as his thumb slowly, mesmerisingly stroked along the back of her hand.

She swallowed a lump of anguish. 'I think you know,' she said. 'This is a game to you. You're here in Australia and you want a playmate. And who better than someone you already know who is going to go away when it's over without too much fuss.'

A corner of his mouth lifted in a rueful smile. 'Your opinion of me is a lot worse than I expected. Didn't I give you enough compensation for bringing an end to our affair?'

More than you know, Bronte thought. 'I sent the opal pendant back,' she said with a defiant glare. 'They're supposed to be bad luck. I kind of figured I had already had my fair share in meeting you.'

A tight spot appeared beside his mouth, like a pulse of restrained anger beating beneath his skin. 'It was very mean-spirited of you to return it in that state,' he said. 'It was an expensive piece. How did you smash it? Did you back over it with an earth mover or something?'

She pushed her chin a little higher. 'I used a hammer. It was immensely satisfying.'

'It was an appalling waste of a rare black opal,' he said. 'If I had known you were going to be so petulant about it I would have given you diamonds instead. They, at least, are unbreakable.'

'I am sure I would have found a way,' she said tightly.

He smiled then, a rare show of perfect white teeth, the movement of his lips triggering the creasing of the fine lines about his eyes. 'Yes, I am sure you would have, *cara.*'

Bronte felt that quivery feeling again and tried desperately to suppress it. What was it about this man that made her so weak and needy? His mere presence made her remember every moment they had spent together. Her body seemed to wake up from a long sleep and leap to fervent life. All her senses were switched to hyper vigilant mode, each and every one of her nerves twitching beneath her skin to be subjected again to the exquisite mastery of his touch.

He had been the most amazing lover. Her *only* lover. She had been romantically and perhaps somewhat foolishly saving herself for the right man. She hadn't wanted to repeat the mistakes her mother had made in falling for a wastrel and then being left holding the baby. Bronte had instead fallen for a billionaire and the baby she had been left holding he still knew nothing about.

And, given how appallingly he had treated her, she planned to keep it that way.

'I have to ask you to leave, Luca,' she said. 'I have a class in a few minutes and I—'

'I want to see you tonight, Bronte,' he stated implacably. 'No is not a word I will tolerate as an answer.'

She pulled out of his hold with a surge of strength that was fuelled by anger. 'You can't force me to do anything, Luca Sabbatini,' she said. 'I am not under any obligation to see you, have dinner with you or even look at you. Now, if you don't leave immediately, I will call the police.'

His dark eyes hardened to black ice. 'How much rent did you say you were paying on this place?' he asked.

Bronte felt a lead-booted foot of apprehension press down on her chest until she could barely breathe. 'I didn't say and I am not going to.'

His smile had a hint of cruelty about it. He reached into the inside breast pocket of his suit jacket and handed her a silver embossed vellum business card. 'My contact details,' he said. 'I will expect you at eight this evening at my hotel. I have written the name and address on the back. I am staying in the penthouse suite.'

'I won't be there,' she warned him as he turned to leave.

He stopped at the door of the studio and turned to look at her. 'Perhaps you had better speak to your previous landlords before you make your final decision,' he said.

'Previous?' Bronte's eyes flared as the realisation dawned. 'You mean you bought the building?' Her heart gave a stutter like an old lawnmower refusing to start. 'Y…you're my new landlord?'

He gave her a self-satisfied smile. 'Dinner at eight, Bronte, otherwise you might find the sudden rise in rent too much to handle.'

Bronte felt anger rise up like lava inside an ancient volcano. Her whole body was shaking with it. Her hands were so tightly fisted her fingers ached, and her blood was pounding so hard in her veins she could hear a roaring in her ears. 'You're *blackmailing* me?' she choked.

He met her excoriating look with equanimity. 'I am asking you on a date, *tesore mio,*' he said. 'You know you want to say yes. The only reason you are making all this fuss is because you are still angry with me.'

'You're damn right I'm still angry with you,' she spat.

'I thought you said you were over me,' he returned with an indolent smile.

Bronte wanted to slap that smile right off his face and only a smidgen of self-discipline and common sense stopped her. 'There is a part of me that will always hate you, Luca,' she said. 'You played with me and then tossed me aside like a toy that no longer interested you. You didn't even have the decency to meet with me face to face to discuss what had gone wrong.'

The hot spot of tension was beating beside his mouth again but Bronte continued regardless. 'What sort of man are you to send one of your lackeys to do your dirty work for you?'

His eyes darkened as he held her burning

gaze. 'I thought it would be less complicated that way,' he said. 'I don't like deliberately upsetting people. Believe me, Bronte, meeting you in person would have been much harder on both of us.'

Bronte rolled her eyes again. 'That is *such* an arrogant thing to say. As if for a moment you had any feelings. You're a heartless, cruel bastard, Luca Sabbatini, and I wish I had never met you.'

The studio door opened again. 'Sorry I'm late. You would not believe the traff— Oh, oops… sorry,' Rachel Brougham said. 'I didn't realise you had company.'

Bronte walked stiffly to the reception desk, using it as a barricade. 'Mr Sabbatini is just leaving,' she said with a pointed glare at Luca.

Rachel's gaze went back and forth like someone at a Wimbledon final. 'You're not one of the parents, are you?' she asked Luca.

'No,' he said with a crooked smile. 'I have not had the pleasure as yet of becoming a father.'

Bronte couldn't look at him. Her face felt like

a furnace as she silently prayed Rachel wouldn't mention Ella.

'So...' Rachel smiled widely, her grey eyes twinkling with interest. 'You know Bronte, huh?'

'Yes,' he said. 'We met a couple of years ago in London. My name is Luca Sabbatini.' He held out his hand to Rachel.

Please, God, please don't let her join the dots, Bronte begged silently.

'Rachel Brougham,' Rachel said, taking his hand and shaking it enthusiastically. 'Hey, I think I read something about you in the paper a couple of weeks ago. You're in hotels, right?'

'That's right,' Luca said. 'I have some business here and thought it would be a good opportunity to catch up again with Bronte. We're planning to have dinner tonight.'

'Actually, I have something on to—' Bronte began.

'She'd love to come,' Rachel said quickly, giving Bronte an are-you-nuts-to-turn-him-down look. 'She hardly ever goes out. I was only telling her the other day how she needs to get a life.'

Bronte sent her friend a look that would have stopped a charging bull in its tracks. Rachel just smiled benignly and turned back to look at Luca. 'So how long are you in Melbourne?' she asked, leaning her elbows on the reception counter as if she was settling in for a good old natter, her expression rapt with interest.

'A month to start with,' he said. 'I will use Melbourne as a base as I have some distant relatives here. I will also be spending a bit of time in Sydney and the Gold Coast.'

Bronte hadn't realised Luca had family here. Although, now that she thought about it, Melbourne had a huge Italian community so it was not all that unlikely he would have cousins or second cousins, even perhaps uncles and aunts. They hadn't really talked too much about their backgrounds when they were involved. Bronte had always found his reticence about his family one of the most intriguing things about him. It was as if he wanted to forget he was from wealth and privilege. He rarely mentioned his work and, although they had dated for six months, he had never flashed his money around as some rich men would have done. They had eaten in nice restaurants, certainly, and, apart from that hideously expensive parting gift delivered by one of his minions, she had never received anything off him other than the occasional bunch of flowers. But then hadn't he unknowingly given her the most priceless gift of all?

'Well, I am sure you'll have a fabulous time while you're in Australia,' Rachel went on, just shy of gushing. 'You speak fabulous English. Have you been here before?'

'Thank you,' Luca said. 'I was educated in England during my teens and have spent the last few years travelling between my homes in Milan and London. I haven't so far had the chance to travel to Australia but both of my brothers have. My older brother's wife is Australian, although they met abroad.'

The first of the afternoon class began to arrive. Bronte watched as Luca turned to look at the group of small children who filed in with their mothers or, in a couple of cases, with their nannies. He smiled softly at them and several mothers did double takes; even the girls beamed up at him as if he was some sort of god or well known celebrity.

'If you'll excuse me,' Bronte said to him stiffly as she moved from behind the reception desk, 'I have a class to conduct.'

'I will see you this evening,' he said, locking gazes with her. 'I have a hire car so I can pick you up if you give me your address.'

Bronte thought of the modest little granny flat she and Ella lived in at the back of her mother's house. She thought too of all the baby paraphernalia that would require an explanation if he was to insist on coming inside. She was not ready to explain anything to him after what he had done. He'd had his chance to find out about his baby and he'd callously thrown it away. 'No, thank you,' she said. 'I can make it on my own.'

He gave her a gleaming smile. 'So you've made up your mind to come after all?'

She gave him a beady look in return. 'It's not as if I have much choice in the matter. You're hanging the threat of charging me an exorbitant rent if I don't comply with your wishes.'

He reached out and trailed the point of his finger down the curve of her cheek, the action setting off a riot of sensation beneath her skin. 'You have no idea what my wishes are, *cara*,' he said softly and, before she could say a word in return, he had turned and left.

CHAPTER TWO

'OF COURSE I'll mind Ella for you,' Tina Bennett said to Bronte later that evening. 'She'll be tucked up in bed in any case by then. Are you going out with Rachel's brother David again? I know he's not exactly your type but he seems a rather sincere sort of chap.'

Bronte cuddled her fourteen-month-old daughter on her lap, breathing in her freshly bathed smell. 'No,' she said, meeting her mother's gaze. 'It's someone I met while I was in London. He's in Melbourne for a few weeks and decided to look me up.'

Tina's slim eyebrows moved together in a worried frown. 'Bronte, darling, is it him? Is it Ella's father?'

Bronte nodded grimly. 'I stupidly thought this day would never come. When he broke off our relationship the message I got was he never wanted to see me again. "A clean break," he said. Now he's suddenly changed the rules.'

'You don't have to see him if you don't want to, darling,' Tina said. 'It's not as if he knows about Ella. Anyway, after the way he treated you, I don't think you are under any obligation to tell him.'

Bronte's long heavy sigh stirred the soft feathery dark brown hair on the top of her baby daughter's head. 'Mum, I've always worried about the timing of it all. He broke things off before I knew I was pregnant. If I had found out just a week earlier it might have changed everything. Perhaps if he had known he might not have been so…so adamant about never seeing me again.'

'Darling, what was a week either side going to do?' her mother asked. 'He had clearly already made up his mind. He wouldn't even agree to talk to you on the phone let alone see you face to face. What were you supposed to do? Tell him via a third party?'

Bronte bit her lip as she looked at her mother. 'Maybe that's what I should have done,' she said. 'Perhaps then he would have agreed to see me again. We could have at least discussed options.'

Tina Bennett gave her daughter a streetwise look. 'And what options might those have been? It's my guess he would have marched you straight off for a termination. A man with that sort of lifestyle would not want a love-child to support. It wouldn't suit his lifestyle.'

'I would never have agreed to that,' Bronte said, holding Ella even closer to her body. 'I would never have allowed anyone to talk me into getting rid of my baby.'

'Darling, you were young and madly in love,' Tina said. 'I know plenty of young women who have done things they later regretted just because the man they loved insisted on it.'

Bronte looked down at her little daughter, who was now snuggling against her chest, her dark blue eyes struggling to stay open as she fought against sleep. It worried Bronte that there might be some truth in what her mother had said. She *had* been young and madly in love. She would have done almost anything to keep Luca by her side. As it was, she had made a pathetic fool of herself chasing after him like a lovesick teenager, leaving countless 'call me' messages and texts on his phone, not to mention pleading emails that made her cringe to think about now.

'You're not going to tell him about Ella, are you, love?' her mother asked.

Bronte gently brushed the soft hair off her sleeping baby's face. 'When he came into the studio unannounced like that today, all I could think was how much I hated him.' She looked up at her mother. 'But one day Ella is going to be old enough to realise she doesn't have a father. She's going to want to know who he is and why he isn't a part of her life. What am I supposed to say? How will I explain it to her?'

'You'll explain it the way I did to you,' her mother said. 'That the man you thought would stay by you deserted you. Remember, Bronte: a father is as a father does. As far as I see it, Luca Sabbatini was nothing more than a sperm donor. One day you'll meet some nice man who will love you and Ella. He will be a far better father to her than a man who cut you from his life without a backward glance. What's to say he does it again if not sooner rather than later? He won't be just hurting you this time, but Ella too.'

'I guess you're right,' Bronte said on a sigh as she rose to her feet, carefully cradling Ella in her arms. 'But there's a part of me that thinks he has a right to know he fathered a child.'

'Men like him don't even like children,' Tina said matter-of-factly. 'They see them as too much responsibility. Believe me, I know the type.'

A small frown tugged at Bronte's brow. 'When my junior class arrived at the studio this afternoon he looked at them…I don't know…almost wistfully, as if he was imagining being a parent one day.'

'Bronte—' her mother's voice sounded stern '—think carefully about this before you do something you might regret. He's a very rich man. A very rich and powerful man. He might take it upon himself to pay you back for not telling him about his child. He could take you to court. You'd have no hope of fighting him and, even if you did, you'd have the burden of paying for the legal work. And, don't forget, given his pedigree background, he would have the best of lawyers at his disposal. The family court is much more accommodating when it comes to fathers these days, especially well-to-do ones. Even if he got partial custody, it would mean Ella would have to fly back and forth to Italy or wherever he currently lives. You might not see her for months on end, and then one day when she's older she might decide not to come back to you at all.'

Bronte felt her heart contract in fear at such an outcome. Luca came from such a powerful dynasty. The Sabbatini clan would be the very worst sort of enemy to take on. Their power and influence reached all over the world. She hadn't a hope in taking Luca on in a custody battle, let alone his family.

The bitter irony was she had never intended to keep Ella's existence a secret. In spite of Luca's insistence that he never wanted to see her again, as soon as Bronte had found out she was pregnant she had tried to contact him. After a couple of fruitless weeks of not getting through to him, she had eventually flown to his villa in Milan but the household staff had refused her entry. The housekeeper had told her rather bluntly that Luca was in America with a new lover.

The news had hit Bronte like a fist in the face. It had devastated her that he had moved on so quickly. She even wondered if he had had his American mistress the whole time he had been seeing her in London. After all, he had never once stayed the full night with her at her flat and he had never allowed her to spend the night with him at his luxurious London home. He had never taken her away for a weekend; she had never even stayed in a hotel with him. He had always insisted on driving her home, his excuse being he was an extremely early riser and didn't want to disturb her. In hindsight, she realised she had been so naïve in accepting his explanation. How gullible of her to have never questioned why he would not spend a single night with her after making love. What sort of lovers didn't spend the night entwined in each other's arms? Street workers and the men who paid them, that was who, Bronte thought bitterly. Luca had treated her like a whore and she had been too blind to see it. But this time she would not be making the same mistake. She would meet him and that would be that. It would be a form of closure for her, something she had longed for when their affair had ended so abruptly. Saying goodbye and meaning it would be very satisfying. She would be finally free of the man who had caused her so much heartache and bitterness, and then and only then would she be able to move on with her life.

Bronte caught a cab to the city rather than worry about parking. She wanted to be able to make a quick escape if things got tricky. She reasoned that an anonymous cab was a much safer exit plan than her battered car with its baby seat full of crumbs and juice stains in the back.

She had dressed for the occasion with deliberate care. Although not exactly destitute, she didn't have the sort of money to throw around that allowed her to fill her wardrobe with designer clothes. But she had a few select items she had bought on sale that made her feel feminine and elegant without being overdressed or too showy.

The hotel was one of the premier ones in the Southbank Complex along the Yarra River. The luxurious marble foyer with a sweeping two-sided staircase with a fountain as its centrepiece gave the hotel more than a touch of Hollywood glamour. Bronte felt like a movie star arriving for a glamorous event as one of the uniformed doormen opened the doors for her with a flourish.

The staircase led to a classy bar area with deep leather sofas placed in intimate formations to give privacy to guests as they socialised over a drink. Bronte saw Luca rise the moment she stepped into the bar. She felt a flutter in her chest as he came towards her and she noted that practically every female head turned to look at him as he moved across the carpeted floor.

He was dressed in a charcoal-grey suit, teamed with a snow-white business shirt and wearing a tie that was red with stripes of silver. He seemed even taller than he had in the studio earlier that day, even though Bronte was now wearing heels.

She felt his gaze move over her, taking in her little black dress, cinched in at the waist with a black patent leather belt which matched her four-inch heels and clutch purse. She was glad she had taken some extra time with her make-up. She had dusted her skin with mineral powder and blush and had made her eyes smoky with eye-shadow and kohl pencil, and her lips ripe and full with a glossy pink lipstick. Her dark brown hair she had smoothed back into a chignon that gave her an added air of sophistication. *Let him look and regret what he threw away,* she thought with a gleam of satisfaction as his pupils flared with male appraisal.

'You are looking quite stunning, *cara*,' he said as he came to stand in front of her, his eyes running over her asssessingly.

She gave him a tight formal smile. 'Let's get this over with, shall we?'

He drew in a breath that pulled at the edges

of his mouth. 'Bronte, there is no need to be so prickly,' he said. 'We are just two old friends catching up, *sì*?'

Bronte's fingers dug into her clutch purse. 'You are no friend of mine, Luca,' she said. 'I think of you as a stupid mistake I made. Something I would like to forget about. I don't like reminding myself of failure.'

His forehead furrowed as he looked down at her. 'It was not you that failed, Bronte. It was my problem. My issues. It was never about you.'

Bronte blinked up at him in surprise. Was that some sort of apology? Or was it part of the softening up process? She was well aware of the Sabbatini charm. It was a lethal potion that could bewitch any unsuspecting woman. And she had not just been unsuspecting but naïve and innocent with it. She had fallen for him so easily. It embarrassed her now to think of how easily. One look, one smile and that bottomless dark chocolate gaze locking on hers had done it. 'So you are prepared to admit you handled things rather callously, are you?' she asked in a wary tone.

He gave her a rueful movement of his lips that fell just short of a smile. 'I have regrets over a lot of things, Bronte. But the past is not something any of us can change. However, I would like to compensate for the hurt I caused you in ending our affair so abruptly and without proper explanation.'

She gave him an embittered look. 'How are you going to compensate me? By blackmailing me into seeing you? It's not working, Luca. You can blackmail me all you like but it won't make me fall in love with you again.'

His dark eyes flickered for a pico-second, a fleeting shadow of something she couldn't identify or understand. 'I realise that is rather a lot to ask after all this time,' he said. 'I would be happy to take it one day at a time, for now.'

Bronte set her mouth. 'You have one evening, Luca, and this is it. I am not doing this again. Say what you have to say and let's leave it at that.'

An arm in arm couple moved past them, the female half turning back to look at Luca. She whispered something to her partner and then he too stopped and stared.

Luca smiled politely but stiffly at the couple and then took Bronte's elbow in the cup of his palm, saying in an undertone, 'Let's get away from the eyes of the public. Before we know it, the press will be tipped off.'

Bronte couldn't bear the thought of being alone with him in his hotel room, but neither could she bear the thought of having her image splashed with his over tomorrow's papers. She could almost imagine the headlines: *Italian hotel tycoon dates ballet teacher single mother.* She would never hear the end of it from the parents of her students, let alone Rachel and her mother.

She followed him to the bank of lifts and silently stepped in beside him as one opened. The doors whooshed closed and she felt as if the air had been cut off along with the background noise of the hotel. It was like being in a capsule with him. The lift was large but it felt like a matchbox with him standing within touching distance. Her stomach gave a nervous quiver. She hadn't been alone with a man since…well, since him. Her one recent date with Rachel's newly divorced older brother had been in a crowded public restaurant. David Brougham hadn't even touched her the whole time they'd worked their way through an eight course degustation menu. *Note to self,* she thought. Never go to a fine dining restaurant with a morose, newly divorced man. Bronte had listened patiently as he had relayed his angst about his marriage breakup and the custodial arrangements for his children, and silently prayed for the evening to be over.

As the lift soared to the penthouse floor Bronte looked at Luca from beneath her lowered lashes. He had a frown of concentration on his fore-head and there were twin lines of tension running either side of his mouth. His arms were hanging by his sides, but she saw him clench and unclench his hands as if he was mentally preparing himself for something.

'I thought you would be used to the intrusion of the media by now,' she said into the humming silence.

He turned his head to look at her. 'Believe me,

Bronte, you never get used to it. Do you know what it's like having every moment of your life documented? The lack of privacy is unbelievable. There are times when I cannot even have a cup of coffee without someone wanting to take a picture. It drives me completely crazy.'

'I guess it's the price of success,' she said. 'You were born into an extremely wealthy family. The public are fascinated by how the other half lives.'

He gave her a quirky smile as the lift stopped at his floor. 'Are *you* fascinated, *cara*?'

She pursed her lips and stepped past him, holding her head at a proud angle. 'You and your family hold no fascination for me whatsoever. I have too much to do in my own life to be keeping track of someone else's.'

As they came to the correct number he inserted his key card into the penthouse suite door and held it open for her to precede him. 'So you haven't kept yourself up to date on all my affairs over the last two years?' he asked.

Bronte spoke without thinking. 'There's been hardly anything about you in the papers and magazines. It always seems to be about your brothers. It's as if you disappeared off the face of the earth the first year after we broke up.'

He gave her a long thoughtful look as he closed the door behind him. 'For a time that's exactly what I wanted to do,' he said, leading the way through to the large lounge. 'What would you like to drink?' he asked over his shoulder.

Bronte was still thinking about why he'd wanted to disappear without trace. There had been something in his tone that seemed tinged with regret and a part of her wondered if it had something to do with her.

Of course not! she chided herself crossly. He was a playboy who had had numerous affairs before she had come along. The only thing that might have set her apart was her innocence and naivety. He had obviously found that a novelty and was hoping for a rerun. She could see it in the dark depths of his eyes every time they meshed with hers. She felt the rush of her blood too, which reminded her rather timely that she was not quite as immune to him as she would have liked.

'Bronte?' he prompted, holding up a bottle of champagne.

'Oh…yes, thanks,' she said, feeling gauche and awkward.

After a moment he handed her a fizzing glass of French champagne, the price of which, Bronte noted, would have paid her last electricity bill, not just for her granny flat but most probably the studio as well.

'To us,' he said, touching his glass against hers.

Bronte hesitated before she took a sip. Luca watched her quizzically, one brow slightly elevated. 'Not to your taste, Bronte?' he asked.

'The champagne, I am sure, is lovely,' she said. 'It's what we're toasting to that is not palatable.'

He held her flinty look with consummate ease. 'You choose, then,' he suggested, holding his glass just in reach of hers. 'What shall we drink to?'

Bronte raised her glass and clinked it against his. 'To moving on.'

His brow went up a little higher this time.

'Interesting,' he said musingly. 'Does this mean the man you are seeing is a permanent fixture in your life?'

Bronte wished she could say yes. And if it was anyone but David Brougham she might well have done so. She felt she needed an excuse, a good excuse, not to see Luca again. It was just too dangerous; not because of Ella, but because of how he made Bronte feel. She could feel emotions bubbling under the surface even now. Dangerous emotions: needs that ached to be fulfilled, longings that wouldn't be suppressed, no matter how hard she tried.

She was supposed to hate him.

She *did* hate him.

He had abandoned her, leaving her when she was so vulnerable and alone. And yet one meeting with him and her mind was filling with images of them together: him kissing her, his lips sealing hers with such passion, his arms around her body, holding her against the surging heat and potency of his. How could she forget how he made her feel? Would there ever be a time when she would not feel her heart twist and ache when she heard his name mentioned or saw it in print? Would she ever be able to forgive him for not loving her, for not even respecting her enough to say goodbye face to face?

'You seem to be taking rather a long time to answer my question,' Luca observed. 'Which can only mean one thing: you are not seriously involved with him. If you were madly in love with someone, surely you would have no hesitation in telling me.'

Bronte drank some of her champagne, stalling for time, for courage, for anything. 'It seems to me it wouldn't matter to you how I answered. You have your own agenda. That's what this little tête à tête is all about, isn't it?'

He wandered over to one of the massive leather sofas and indicated for her to sit down. He waited until she was perched on the edge of one of the cushions before he spoke. 'I want to see you, Bronte. Not just tonight. Not even just now and again.' He waited a beat, his eyes intense and unwavering on hers. 'I want to see you as much as possible while I am here. I want you back.'

Bronte's hand trembled as she held the champagne glass. She tried to hold it steady by cradling it with both of her hands, her heart beating like an out of time pendulum. 'I…you…I… I'm afraid that's not possible…' she faltered.

He came to sit beside her, his hand removing the glass from her shaking ones. 'I mean it, *cara*,' he said and took both of her hands in his warm, dry ones. 'I have never forgotten you.'

Bronte felt anger come to her rescue. She wrenched out of his hold and jumped to her feet. 'I am not some stupid plaything you can pick up and put down when you feel like it,' she said. 'You were the one to end things. You wanted a clean break and you got one. Coming back after all this time and telling me you've changed your mind is not just arrogant, it's downright insulting.'

Luca rose to his feet and pushed a hand through his hair. 'Bronte, I wasn't ready for a relationship two years ago. You came along at the wrong time. God, how I wish I could have met you just a year later. Even six months later. Everything would have been so different then.'

She glowered at him and he felt a spike go through his chest. He had not expected her to hate him quite so much. This was going to be a little harder than he'd expected but he was prepared to work hard for what he wanted. If there were obstacles in the way he would remove them. If there was a way of winning her back to him he would do it, even if he had to resort to ruthless means. He had hoped he would not have to apply any sort of pressure. The rent thing was an insurance scheme on his part to get this far. First base was to see her again in private. He hadn't even thought as far as second and third. He had just so desperately wanted to see her again.

Bronte was still sending him looks with daggers and spears attached. 'So what brought about this sudden change, Luca?' she asked.

Should he tell her? Luca wondered. He had told no one; not even his mother or brothers or elderly grandfather had known the truth about his trip to America until the deed was over and he was safely on the other side. He hadn't wanted his family to go through the agonising heartache of knowing they could lose him or, even worse, have him come back to them damaged beyond recognition. He had seen his father propped up in a semi-conscious state in the last weeks before he'd finally died from the injuries he had sustained in a head-on collision. That had decided it for him. He had wanted to spare his mother and brothers from witnessing anything as gut-wrenching as that.

Luca hated talking about that time, now that it was over. He liked to push it to the back of his mind, inside a locked compartment inside his brain. In the weeks and months afterwards he would creak it open almost daily, marvelling that he was still here, functioning and breathing and talking. Now he just wanted to forget it had ever happened. The shame of his body letting him down so cruelly was something he no longer wanted to mull over. Telling Bronte about it would only make it come back to haunt him. It was too personal and too private and there was no way he could risk anything being leaked to the press if she wanted to try her hand at a payback. It was better she didn't know. He just wanted his life to begin again from now. He was ready to move on and he wanted to do so with a clean slate.

'I am at a time of life when I am looking for more stability,' he said. 'What we had was good, Bronte. Some of the happiest times of my life were those I spent with you.'

Her slate-blue eyes were dark with suspicion. 'Were those good times just with me, Luca? Or are you getting me mixed up with someone else?'

'I never betrayed you, *cara*,' he said. 'There was only you during that time. No one else.'

Her eyes rolled upwards as she swung away from him, her arms doing that barricade thing across her slim body, warning him off, shutting him out. 'You betrayed me by ending our relationship without a single explanation as to why,' she said in an embittered tone.

Luca took a deep breath, holding it for a few seconds before he slowly released it. 'I never intended to hurt you the way I did, Bronte. I accept full responsibility for it. I know it's hard for you to understand, but I had no choice. It was not the time for us. We met too soon.'

She turned back to look at him, her expression so scathing it actually hurt him to maintain eye contact. 'So, now you've sown all your wild oats, you want what, exactly?' she asked. 'You're not proposing marriage, are you?'

Luca was not going to offer something that would be thrown back in his face, or at least not yet. There were other ways to bring about what he wanted. More subtle ways. 'No,' he said. 'I am not proposing anything long-term at this stage. I am here in your country and I would like to see if what we had before can be resurrected.'

Her lips pressed so tightly together they went white. After a tense moment she expelled her held breath on a whoosh. 'You are unbelievable,' she said. 'You think you can just pick up where you left off, all things forgiven? What planet did you just drop down from? As if I would agree to being involved with you again. *As if!*'

It was the tone of her 'As if' that did it. Luca

felt his temper snap to attention like an elastic band stretched to the limit. 'You might not have any choice in the matter,' he said.

Her eyes flared as his words hit home. 'You wouldn't dare...' She almost breathed rather than said the words.

He pushed his jaw forward, his eyes locked on hers. 'I want you back in my bed, Bronte. If you don't agree then there is nothing more to be said between us. You will have one week to vacate the premises of your studio. If you don't vacate in one week the rent will increase substantially.'

Her soft mouth fell open, her eyes still as wide as saucers. 'You can't mean that...' she swallowed and then swallowed again, her voice coming out even scratchier '...y...you can't possibly mean that...'

Luca came over to her and stood just within touching distance, his eyes pinning hers. 'The decision is yours, Bronte,' he said, running a hand down her upper arm from shoulder to elbow, each and every pore of her flesh rising in shivery goosebumps under his touch. 'Which is it to be?'

CHAPTER THREE

BRONTE couldn't think. Her mind was whirling like a fairground ride that had been set at too fast a speed. He wanted her to sleep with him. He wanted to resume their affair. He didn't want anything permanent. He was going to use her and discard her like he did before. Round and round the thoughts went until she felt dizzy and sick and heartsore. How could he do this to her? He was the one who had walked away. It wasn't as if she had done anything to hurt him. He had broken her heart, he had all but ruined her life and yet here he was acting as if she owed him!

She stepped back from him, biting the inside of her mouth until she tasted blood. She turned on her heel and began pacing the floor. She had to think of a way out of this. *Was* there a way out of this?

'Come here.'

Bronte felt his two word command like hammer blows to her heart. How ruthless he sounded! She was nothing but a chattel, a possession he had bartered for. She stopped pacing and stood her ground, her chin high, with her eyes flashing their hatred at him. 'If you want me then you'll have to drag me kicking and screaming for I will not come willingly.'

His lips slowly curved upwards in a sexy smile. 'Are you absolutely sure about that, *tesore mio*?' he asked in a low husky drawl.

Now that you mention it, Bronte thought in panic as she recalled his warm electrifying touch on her arm just moments ago. He had set spot fires all throughout her body with that one stroke of his hand along her upper arm. He had awakened every nerve of her skin, made her heart beat twice its pace and made a hole open up deep inside her, a hollow ache she knew from experience could only be filled by him.

He came back to where she was standing; actually, shaking was probably a more accurate description. He placed a broad fingertip beneath her rigid chin and slowly but surely lifted it until her eyes had nowhere to go but meet his. 'It's still there, isn't it, *cara*?' he said. 'The chemistry between us. I felt it the moment I walked into the studio this afternoon. I can feel it now. You can too. I can see it in your eyes. I can feel it when I touch you. You tremble all over.'

Bronte stopped breathing when he brought his mouth to the corner of hers. He brushed his lips against her skin, a feather-light touch that made her quiver in reaction, fulfilling every word he had just spoken about her response to him. Her body was her betrayer; she had no hope of disguising how he affected her. His warm hint-of-mint breath skated over her lips before touching down on the other side of her mouth, the same soft brush of lips on sensitive skin evoking the same heady rush of feeling inside her body. She heard a soft whimper and realised with a little jolt it had come from her mouth. Her lips had softly fallen open, her mouth an open invitation for the plunder of his.

But he didn't do it.

He smiled that lazy smile as he met her

bewildered, uncertain gaze and then he slowly pressed a soft barely-there kiss to each of her eyebrows. 'You have the most amazing blue eyes,' he said, low and deep like a bolt of satin dragged across gravel. 'Like the heart of a flame, dark and fiery. They burn one minute and the next they shine like the surface of a deep ocean.'

She trembled all over as he ran his hands down both of her arms, his fingers encircling her wrists like handcuffs. She felt the soft tug that brought her flat against his body, her belly coming into contact with his arousal. Heat exploded inside her, pooling between her thighs, hot and fragrant with need. How could she still want him when she hated him so much? It didn't seem fair that her body would betray her so shamelessly. She hated herself for being so weak. She hated him for making her want him. She hated that she wanted to lean into him and offer her mouth and body to his to pleasure. The pressure of want was building deep inside her: an ache, a pulse, a drumbeat that would not be ignored.

'Beautiful, sweet Bronte,' he said just above her mouth. 'Do you have any idea how much I still want you?'

Bronte felt the proud probe of his hot hard flesh and felt an answering quake of want in her inner core. It was like a hungry beast growling for satiation inside her. Her body stepped up its demand for assuagement, torturing her with tiny exquisite reminders of the pleasure she had felt with him in the past. Her mind was full of images of them locked in erotic poses: his body pinning her from above, from below, from behind or up against the nearest wall or even on the kitchen counter, his body pounding into hers, her arms locked around his neck or waist, her body coming apart time and time again.

'Tell me you feel it too,' he said just above her mouth, his warm breath a caress, a temptation, a torture. 'Tell me you remember how it was between us.'

Bronte was beyond speech. She just wanted to feel his mouth on hers, even if it was for the last time. Surely it wasn't wrong to want that? Just a taste, a reminder of how it felt to have him kiss her senseless. She pulled her hands out of the loose grasp of his and linked them around his neck. She looked him in the eyes, drowning all over again in their dark brown depths. And then she rose up on tiptoe and pressed her mouth to his, somehow knowing that in doing so she was passing a point of no return.

It was like fire meeting fuel. A burn of longing that flickered and then roared, consuming everything in its path. Her mouth opened at the first searing, searching thrust of his tongue, her tongue dancing with his, darting away shyly at first and then flirting with his outrageously, boldly, wantonly. He groaned deeply as he deepened the kiss, his hands guiding her body as he backed her up against the nearest wall, his mouth increasing its pressure, its heat and its passion until she felt as if she was being sucked into a whirlpool of clawing, desperate need.

With the wall at her back, his body had more leverage against hers. She felt the hard ridge of him against her belly, the pounding heat of his blood surging through his veins in primal response to his need to mate. She felt the urge too.

It was beating inside her like a primitive tribal drum, the walls of her feminine core quivering in anticipation of the delicious friction of his commanding possession.

His mouth was like a naked flame against hers. His kiss was scorching her but she returned it with matching heat, her tongue darting and diving in a cat and mouse game with his. His hands slid up her body and cupped her breasts, gently but possessively, his thumbs claiming her erect nipples as his own to pleasure, to caress and to tease into submission.

Bronte arched up against him shamelessly. She wished she could rip her clothes off in one movement to feel his warm masculine hands on her bare skin. She tugged at his shirt, pulling it free of his trousers, sliding her hands up his chest, her fingers exploring the hard musculature that had delighted her so much in the past. She felt the hard, flat nubs of his nipples and the scratchy dusting of masculine hair over his chest. He was in every way possible a man: strong and capable, lean but hard muscled, fit and virile, potent and irresistibly sexy.

His mouth moved from hers to her breast; the hot moist feel of him caressing her made her spine turn to liquid. She made a soft sound in the back of her throat, something between a whimper and a gasp.

'I have dreamed of doing this,' Luca said throatily. 'Touching you, feeling you respond to me. No one else has ever turned me on quite like you do.'

It was just the reminder Bronte needed that she was not the only one he had been with and she was certainly not going to be the last. He had worked his way through a glamorous array of women since he was a teenager. She had known of his playboy reputation when she first met him but somehow hadn't been able to resist his seductive charm. She was older and wiser now. And she had responsibilities. Ella was her most important one. There was nothing she would not do to protect her baby girl. Denying herself this was a sacrifice she had to make. For now, at least, until she could find a way out of the honey trap Luca had lured her into.

She let her hands drop from around his neck,

her eyes meeting his. 'I can't do this, Luca,' she said. 'Not here. Not like this. It's…it's too soon.'

His eyes seared hers for an endless moment, a muscle working in his jaw as he fought to control his rampant desire. 'Remember our deal,' he said.

Bronte slipped out from his arms where they were propped against the wall either side of her head and put a little distance between their bodies. She struggled to get her breathing to steady, difficult when her pulse was fluttering like a hummingbird inside her veins.

'Deal?' she asked with a scornful look. 'Don't you mean the bribe you put on the table, Luca? Money for sex.'

'That is rather a crude way of putting it,' he said.

'It's the truth, though, isn't it?' she asked. 'You want to turn me into a whore. You open your wallet; I open my legs. That's the so-called deal, isn't it?'

A nerve ticked like a pulse at the side of

his mouth. 'Don't cheapen yourself like that, Bronte.'

Bronte gave a choked laugh that was just shy of hysteria. 'You tell me not to cheapen myself when you have insulted me more than any other person I know.'

He drew in a breath and moved across the room, standing at the windows that overlooked the shimmering lights of the city below. Bronte saw the stiff set to his broad shoulders, the straight spine and the long legs standing slightly apart.

She longed to go to him and wrap her arms around him, to take whatever he was offering, but she knew in the end it would only lead to further heartbreak. How could she ever trust he wouldn't walk out on her again? She would not survive it a second time. It had nearly done her in the first time. It had only been the responsibility of Ella that had made her come to her senses and grow up—and grow up fast. But, even so, it was tempting. Oh, dear God, it was tempting. To feel his arms around her one more time, to have him hold her as if she was the most precious thing in the entire world. How she had dreamed and longed for one more time with him over the last two years.

'Fine,' he said after a long moment, his voice sounding hollow and empty. 'You are free to go.'

Bronte felt her heart give a little start. 'But I thought—'

He turned, his dark eyes hitting hers. 'Go, Bronte. Before I change my mind.'

She swallowed and took a hesitant step towards the door, but then she remembered her clutch purse was sitting on the sofa. She glanced at it but, before she could move, he stepped forward and picked it up.

He came over to where she was standing and handed it to her. 'This is all wrong, isn't it?' he said.

She rolled her lips against each other, not sure if he wanted an answer or not. Of course it was wrong. It was wrong for her to still want him, no matter what terms he laid down. It was shameless of her, needy and pathetic and desperate, but that was what he reduced her to. No man had ever made her feel so desperately in need. No man had made her heart ache with an indescribable longing. No man had made her want to throw herself at him in spite of everything.

She had to leave.

She had to leave *now*, before he saw how close she was to offering herself for further hurt. She had to leave before these minutes alone turned into an hour or two of stolen pleasure that, just like in the past, would trick her too-trusting, too-romantic mind into thinking they had any sort of future.

'I have handled this all wrong,' he said again with a rueful tilt to his mouth. 'I should have called you first, given you some warning, perhaps. Maybe then you would not be so wary of me. You would have been better prepared, *sì*?'

'Why didn't you?' she asked in a scratchy voice.

One of his broad shoulders rose and fell. 'I wanted to see your instinctive response to me, not a rehearsed one.'

Bronte gave him a disdainful look. 'You make it sound like some sort of social experiment.'

His eyes stayed on hers: dark, tempting, fathomless. 'I would like to see you again, *cara*,' he said. 'Tomorrow night. No strings this time. No threats or bribes or blackmail, just two people having dinner together. If you like, we can pretend we have met for the first time.'

Bronte chewed at her lip, torn between temptation and uncertainty. Was this some sort of set-up? What if he still wanted to pull the financial rug from under her feet? 'The rent thing...' she said. 'I don't have that sort of money. I think you know that.'

'Forget about the rent,' he said. 'I don't want you in my bed because you have no choice in the matter. I know you will come to me, Bronte. It is inevitable. I knew that as soon as I walked into the studio.'

Had she been that transparent? Bronte wondered. 'You are deluding yourself, Luca,' she said with a proud hitch of her chin. 'You mistook surprise for something else.'

His knowing half-smile travelled all the way to

his eyes. 'So beautiful,' he said, trailing a slow-moving finger down the curve of her cheek. 'So very beautiful.'

Bronte flinched in case she betrayed herself completely. His touch was like a feather and yet it set every nerve screaming for more. 'What's going on, Luca?' she asked, rubbing at her cheek as if he had tainted her.

His expression was like a blank stone wall. 'What do you mean?'

'This…' She waved her arm to encompass the suite. 'You. Me. Us. I'm not sure what's really going on. I get the feeling there is far more to this than you're telling me.'

He gave her a small twisted smile. 'Is it so hard for you to understand I wanted to see you again? Would it not have seemed strange for me to travel all this way, knowing you lived in the same city where I would be based and not at least try and make contact with you?'

Bronte's mouth tightened with cynicism. 'Do you make contact with *all* your ex-lovers wherever you travel in the world? If so, I am sure by now your little black book would be classified as overweight luggage.'

His smile lingered for a moment as if he found the thought amusing. 'There have not been as many lovers as you might think,' he said. 'I have been busy with...other things.'

Bronte wondered what *other things* had taken up his time. She knew he worked hard in the family business but he had found plenty of time in the past to play hard too. If he wasn't squiring yet another wannabe model or Hollywood starlet like his equally single younger brother Nicoló, what had he been doing?

'Did you drive here or catch a cab?' Luca asked.

'I caught a cab,' she said. 'I didn't want to have to worry about parking.'

He reached for a set of car keys on a nearby sideboard. 'I'll drive you home.'

Bronte felt a frisson of fear run through her like a trickle of ice-cold water. 'You don't have to do that,' she said quickly. 'I mean...it's no trouble getting a cab. I would prefer it, actually...'

His eyes narrowed just a fraction. 'What is the

problem, Bronte? You surely trust me to get you home safely? I do know which side of the road to drive on here.'

'It's not that,' she said. 'I would prefer to make my own arrangements.'

'Is there someone waiting for you at home?' he asked.

'My private life has nothing to do with you, Luca,' she said. 'Not any more.'

He continued to watch her, his eyes dark and inscrutable. He didn't speak, which made the silence open up like a chasm between them.

'Look,' Bronte finally said, moving from foot to foot with impatience, 'I have to work tomorrow. And I don't want my mother to worry.'

'Your mother?' A deep frown appeared between his brows. 'You live with your mother?'

She straightened her spine. 'What's wrong with that?' she asked. 'Property is horrendously expensive in Melbourne. I can't afford the studio rent and a mortgage. I'm just starting out.'

'How long have you been teaching at the studio?' he asked, still frowning.

'About a year,' Bronte said. 'Rachel and I

trained at the same academy together. She broke her ankle in a car accident a couple of years ago and had to give up dancing. We decided to set up our own ballet school.'

Another silence passed but to Bronte it felt like hours. Each second seemed weighted; even the air seemed heavy and too thick for her to breathe.

'The audition you said you missed,' he said, watching her steadily. 'Did that by any chance have anything to do with me?'

Bronte felt her heart trip and carefully avoided his gaze. 'W...why do you ask that?'

'We broke up, what, about four weeks before you were due to audition, right?'

She gave a could-mean-anything shrug and fiddled with the catch on her clutch purse. 'I didn't see the point in trying for the company when my heart wasn't in staying in London,' she said. She brought her gaze back up to his. 'It was time for me to go home, Luca. There was nothing in London for me. The competition was tough, in any case. I didn't have a hope of making the shortlist. The audition would have been yet another rejection I just wasn't up to facing.'

'So you preferred to not show up at all rather than to fail.' It was not a question but a rather good summation of what she had been feeling at the time.

Bronte hadn't realised he had known her quite so well. She hadn't spoken to him of her doubts about making the grade. Their relationship hadn't been the sort for heart-to-heart confessions. She had always felt as if he was holding himself at a distance, not just physically but emotionally, so she had done the same. 'Yes,' she said, deliberately holding his gaze. 'I did, however, speak to the head of auditions in person and explain I was withdrawing my application. I had at least the common decency to do that.'

There was another long drawn-out silence.

'I know you took it hard, Bronte,' he said in a husky tone. 'I didn't want to hurt you but I am afraid it was unavoidable. I had to end it. I had no other choice.'

Bronte blinked back the smarting of tears. She was *not* going to cry in front of him. She had cried all the tears she was ever going to cry over him two years ago. 'Was there someone else the whole time?' she asked in a cool crisp tone. 'You can be honest with me, Luca. I am a big girl now. I can take it. I wasn't enough to satisfy you, was I? I wasn't worldly enough for your sophisticated tastes.'

He gave her a brooding frown. 'Is that what you thought?'

She flattened her mouth. 'It's what I know,' she said. 'I was a novelty for you at first but it must have become annoying after a while. I was good enough to have sex with but not good enough for you to take on any of your trips abroad. But no doubt you had plenty of women to step into my place.'

He continued to frown at her. 'That is not the way it was, Bronte.' He raked one of his hands through his hair, making it look as if he had just tumbled out of bed. 'I've always preferred to travel alone. It's less complicated.'

Bronte bit the inside of her mouth to control her spiralling emotions. Why hadn't she left five minutes ago before it had got to this? 'We went out for close to six months,' she said. 'Not once did you spend a whole night with me. Not once, Luca. You never even took me for a weekend away. Not even into the country. I was your city mistress. The easy girl you could bed any time you liked. You only had to pick up the phone and I was available.'

Luca came over and captured Bronte's flailing hands, holding them firmly in his grasp. 'Stop it, Bronte,' he said. 'You were no such thing. Not to me.'

She looked at him with tears shining in her eyes. 'You used me, Luca. You can't deny it. You used me and when you got tired of me you let me go.'

Luca looked down at her hands, struggling to get away from his. His hands were so olive-skinned and dark and big compared to her slim, small creamy ones. Her hands reminded him of small doves fluttering to get away. Her body was so slight. Everything about her was so dainty and elegant. Her dancer's body, the way she carried herself, the way her eyes looked so big and dark in the perfect oval of her face.

He looked into those big dark eyes and wondered how he could repair the damage he had done. He could see the pain his rejection had caused. It glimmered there amongst the sheen of tears she was so determined not to shed in front of him.

She was so unlike any other woman he had been with in the past. He had loved the fact he was her first lover. She had seemed embarrassed about it but he had secretly delighted in it. He wondered if that was why he could not forget her. She had touched him in a way no one else had ever done. There was a place deep inside of him no one had ever been able to reach and yet he had felt as if she had come so very close. He had not wanted to fall in love with anyone, not with his health the way it had been back then. But with Bronte he had come close. Too close. That was why he'd had to back off before he was in so deep he wouldn't be able to think rationally. The more time he'd spent with her, the more he'd realised how unfair it would be on her to tie her to him when there was no guarantee he could give her anything in return.

Luca released one of her hands so he could put his other hand in the small of her back, bringing her up against him again. He loved the feel of her body flush against his. She fitted against him as if she had been made for him. He felt his body stirring and wished he could show her what he found so hard to say out loud. But it would only scare her away. It was too soon. He had to take things slowly and carefully this time. She was like a shy fawn with an innate sense of danger. She needed time and careful handling. He had the patience for the careful handling, but time was something he didn't have at his disposal. A month was all he had to get her to come back to him, to see if the magic was still there so they could build some sort of future together. Would it be enough?

'Don't fight me, Bronte,' he said softly. 'You are angry at me and I know I deserve it, but we still have something between us. You know we do.'

Her eyes flared like a cornered animal facing a dangerous predator. 'W…we share nothing,' she stammered. 'I don't want to see you. I don't want to be your sex slave. I don't want to be your…your anything.'

He brought her other hand to his mouth, kissing each of her stiff fingertips until he felt them tremble against his lips. He kept his eyes trained on hers, watching as the point of her tongue darted out nervously to anoint her lips. 'I am not asking you to be anything but my partner for dinner tomorrow evening,' he said.

She swallowed tightly. 'And…and after that?'

He kissed the backs of her bent knuckles, still holding her gaze. 'If you don't want to see me again I will have to accept it,' he said.

Her eyes narrowed in suspicion. 'You'll let me go? Just like that?'

Luca stroked away the frown that had appeared between her brows. 'If you frown all the time you will get wrinkles.'

She arched her head away from his touch. 'You didn't answer my question, Luca.'

Luca let out a sigh as he dropped his hand back by his side. 'I didn't have to blackmail you into my bed in the past,' he said. 'I don't see why I should need to do so now.'

Her chin came up and her eyes flashed blue fire at him. 'So you think I'll just dive in head first then, do you?'

He examined her taut expression for a moment or two. 'I think what will happen will happen, *cara*,' he said. 'We should leave things to fate, *sì*?'

She continued to regard him warily. 'Fate, huh? Like it's fate that you're suddenly my landlord.'

'You're not in any danger of being kicked out on the street,' Luca said.

'Can I have that in writing?' she asked.

He stood looking down at her for a long moment, breathing in her scent, that hint of honeysuckle and sun-warmed sweet peas that unfurled inside his nostrils, making them flare to take more of her in. 'You really don't trust me, do you?'

She folded her arms across her chest. 'No, strange as it may seem, I don't trust you. I don't like you and I can't wait to see the last of you.'

Luca felt his spine tighten with irritation. Did she have to keep reminding him of how much she hated him? Did she think it would make him want her less? If anything, it made him want her more. Or was that her intention? Was she playing hard to get to teach him a lesson, or to get more out of the relationship this time around? Maybe the last couple of years had toughened her up. Maybe she had enrolled in the academy of gold-diggers and now knew how to use men to serve her own ends. Either way, it didn't matter. He wanted her any way he could get her. If she had changed, well, so had he. He was not the same person he had been two years ago. How could he be? Too much had happened.

He went over to where he had put their champagne glasses down before. He picked up her glass and brought it back to where she was standing. 'It would be a shame to let such good champagne go to waste,' he said, offering it to her. 'Why not stay a few minutes more and help me finish it?'

She looked at the glass as if he was handing her a poisoned chalice.

'It's just champagne, Bronte,' he said. 'Let's finish our drink and catch up on the last two years.' He took a sip from his glass, hoping she would follow suit. Anything to prolong the time he had with her in case she didn't show up tomorrow. 'Tell me about your teaching. Do you enjoy it?'

She took a tiny sip of her champagne and then held the glass with both of her hands around the stem. 'I do, yes,' she said. 'The children are lovely.'

He patted the sofa, indicating for her to sit down. She sat on the edge of the seat again, ready for instant flight. 'How many students do you have?' he asked, trying to put her at ease.

'We have sixty at the moment but I would like to see it go to about two hundred,' she said. 'I have plans for extension of classes. I would like to hire a couple more teachers for jazz and tap, and I want to incorporate some adult classes.'

Luca took a sip of his champagne. 'You teach adults?' he asked. 'Isn't it too late for an adult to learn? I thought ballet was something you had to learn at a very young age, the younger the better.'

'That's true, but there are lots of women and some men, when it comes to that, who have studied dance in the past and have let it slip,' she said. 'Doing a weekly or twice weekly class with other adults is a good way of keeping in shape.'

Luca let his eyes run over her slim form. 'Yes, well, it certainly hasn't done you any harm,' he said with a crooked smile. 'You're as slim as ever. How often do you practice?'

A light blush shaded her cheeks and she looked down at the contents of her glass again. 'A couple of hours a day,' she said. 'I would like to do more but with El...' She stopped mid-sentence and sank her teeth in her lip before continuing falteringly, '...I mean with every-thing there is to do around here I...I haven't got a lot of time.'

Luca watched as her colour deepened even further. She reminded him of a shy schoolgirl, nervous, timid, not sure of herself in spite of all of her talent. It was so endearing he felt as if a large hand was pressing down on his heart. He thought of all the streetwise women who had thrown themselves at him in the past. They had used their looks and glamour and wily ways to get his attention. Bronte, on the other hand, had done nothing of the sort. She had always been reserved and held a lot of herself back. It made him all the more determined to draw her out of herself. She was such a rare find, so pure and unblemished. Like a rare diamond.

She got up from the sofa and put the glass down. 'I'm sorry, Luca, but I have to go.'

'What's the hurry?' he asked, rising to his feet.

She turned and faced him, her gaze quickly falling away from his as she searched again for her clutch purse. 'My mother will be wondering what's keeping me. I said I was only going out for a quick drink.'

'Bronte, you are twenty-five years old,' he pointed out. 'Do you really have to check in and out with your mother as if you were fifteen?'

Her eyes gave him a hard little glare. 'My

mother has been very good to me. She has stood by me and supported me unconditionally. I don't have to answer to her, but I choose to out of respect for all the sacrifices she has made for me.'

'Surely she won't begrudge you a night out,' he said. And then, after a beat, added with a curl of his lip, 'Or has it more to do with this other man you're seeing?'

She sent him a challenging look. 'What if it does?'

Luca felt a rush of jealousy hit him like a tsunami. His stomach clenched as he thought of her with another man. His skin broke out in a sickening sweat as he imagined them together. He felt nauseous thinking about it. He didn't want to think about it. He *wouldn't* think about it. 'What is his name?' he asked in a cool unaffected tone when inside his guts were churning.

Her small chin rose. 'I don't have to tell you.'

Luca put his glass down before he snapped the fragile stem. He surreptitiously clenched and unclenched his hands, fighting for control.

She was deliberately goading him, dangling her lover in front of him like a red rag to a raging bull. 'Are you sleeping with him?' he asked, not wanting to know but asking anyway.

'That is none of your business.'

He watched as she snatched up her purse, which had slipped down between the loose cushions of the sofa. She clipped it shut and stalked to the door, throwing over her shoulder, 'Thank you for the drink. Goodbye.'

'We have a date for tomorrow,' he reminded her.

She stiffened as if she had been snap-frozen from head to foot. 'I won't be able to make it,' she said, not bothering to turn around and face him.

'Damn it, Bronte, I am only asking for one night,' he said in rising frustration. 'Is that so very much to ask?'

She turned then, slowly, meeting his eyes with a glare of deep, bottomless blue anger in her own. 'Yes, Luca, it is too much to ask. You never gave me a single night of your time the whole time we were together.'

Luca felt his jaw snap together like a steel trap. His teeth ached with the pressure of forming the words to speak. 'So this is payback, is it?'

'No, Luca,' she said, opening the door. 'This is justice.'

And then she shut the door in his face.

CHAPTER FOUR

Luca didn't find the mobile phone until an hour after Bronte had gone. He had paced the floor in anger for half an hour before he stopped to pour himself another drink from the barely touched bottle of champagne.

He took the bottle and his glass over to the sofa where Bronte had been sitting earlier. He tossed the first glass down and then poured himself another, barely tasting it before he swallowed. Right at this moment he didn't care if he got drunk. It would certainly be preferable to this.

He swore viciously and pushed his hair back off his forehead. He had hoped the night would have turned out differently but he had obviously been fooling himself. Bronte was well and truly over him. She had walked out and made it clear she wasn't coming back. He had hoped she still felt something for him. It was a wild hope, a vain, perhaps even an arrogant hope, but a hope all the same.

She had taken a long time to admit to loving him but when she had finally said it he knew she had meant it. Back then he hadn't been entirely sure if what he felt for her was love; all he knew was he felt different when he was with her, unlike he had ever felt before. But at that time he hadn't been sure he had a future to offer her. So he had kept his feelings to himself. He knew he had often come across as cold emotionally. He was often irritable and short-tempered with her on the days after he had been unwell and, while he knew it had confused her and made her feel insecure, he had never told her why he was feeling out of sorts. He hadn't wanted her to feel obligated towards him. She was the sort of person who would sacrifice herself and he hadn't been prepared for her to do that. It was his burden, his cross to bear and he had borne it and finally, thank God, got rid of it.

He reached forward to pour himself another glass of champagne, when something hard pressed against his thigh. He looked down and saw a slimline black mobile phone poking up through the cushions.

He smiled a slow smile as he pulled it out. It was the same model as his, only his was the newer upgraded one. He turned it over in his hand, pressing the silent switch on the side to ringtone. It immediately buzzed with messages; one by one they came up on the screen. It was impossible not to read them, even if his conscience told him it was an invasion of privacy.

How did it go?
What's he like?
Did you tell him about you know who?
Call me!!!!!

Luca scrolled past the other icons, but his finger stilled on the photo gallery one. He hesitated for a fraction of a moment before he pressed it to open it. There were a lot of pictures of a baby girl. He couldn't determine the age but he thought she was under one year old. She was small, like a doll, with dark brown hair and big blue eyes.

His gut seized and his hand shook as he scrolled through a couple more photos. She was a miniature version of Bronte. She was still in nappies; it looked as if she had only just started to walk. Luca felt a pain like a thick metal skewer go through the middle of his heart. He hadn't been expecting this. He hadn't seen it coming. He felt a fool for not realising. No wonder she didn't want anything more to do with him. Bronte had well and truly moved on with her life.

She'd had a baby.

She'd had another man's child.

The knowledge was too painful. His chest cavity felt too tight, suddenly too small to accommodate his organs. He couldn't breathe without pain. Each breath was like a knife between his ribs. His lungs felt as if they were going to explode.

He couldn't bear to look at any more pictures. He couldn't trust himself not to smash the phone if he came across the child's father in one of them. He didn't want to know who it was or what he looked like. No doubt it was some solidly dependable suburban type who had swept Bronte off her feet and offered her the security she longed for. Luca hadn't noticed a wedding ring on her finger but having a child with someone these days often came first. She had said she lived with her mother but did her lover and the father of her child live there too? No wonder she hadn't wanted him to pick her up or even know where she lived. *Dio*, he couldn't bear the thought of her going home to lie in someone else's arms. Even now she could be making love with the father of her child, perhaps conceiving another one with him right at this very moment.

His fingers clenched around the phone as he laid his head back against the sofa cushions. He closed his eyes tightly, almost painfully, trying to block out the taunting images his brain concocted, thinking instead of how a few months could have changed everything.

The phone began to vibrate in his hand.

Luca opened his eyes and looked down at the screen. He slid the answer arrow across and held the phone up to his ear. 'Hello.'

There was a short silence marked by some rapid breathing.

'Luca?'

'Bronte,' Luca drawled, idly crossing one ankle over his thigh. 'How nice of you to call.'

Another tight silence.

'You have my phone.' The words came out like small, hard pellets. 'It must have slipped out of my purse or something.'

'Yes, it must have,' he said. 'You want to come and get it or shall I bring it to dinner tomorrow night?'

'I...'

'Or I could bring it around to your place now,' he said.

'No!'

Luca curled his lip, trying to ignore the pain in his gut. 'It would be no trouble, Bronte. Where do you live?'

'I don't want you to come here, Luca,' she said stiffly.

'Lover boy wouldn't like it?' he asked.

The silence this time crackled with tension.

'I need my phone,' she said. 'I will come and get it now...if that's all right? I mean if it's not too late or anything.'

Luca glanced at his watch and smiled. 'I'll be waiting for you.'

The call ended and he tapped his fingers against the phone where it rested on his thigh, his smile disappearing as a heavy frown pulled at his forehead.

Bronte pulled into the hotel's arrival bay and reluctantly left the keys with the valet parking attendant. She had tried to explain she wouldn't be long but hotel policy forbade parking out the front, even for short intervals. The tense exchange of words with the attendant on duty hadn't improved her already overstretched nerves. The moment of panic when she'd realised she had left her phone behind had practically sent her heart into a fibrillation. A heart attack at twenty-five was unlikely but Bronte felt as if she was going to go very close.

Had Luca looked at the photos of Ella? There were literally dozens of them. Fortunately there were none of Ella's firstborn ones or any from the first few months of her life. Bronte had transferred all her photos only a couple of weeks ago so she only had more recent photos on it.

But even so...

Would Luca see the likeness? Her mother had assured her it was unlikely. Ella was small for her age and had the same hair colour as Bronte and the same slate-blue eyes, dainty features and creamy skin.

Bronte wasn't so sure her mother was right, however. At times she could see a lot of Luca in her daughter. When Ella was concentrating over a puzzle or a toy she couldn't quite figure out, she frowned just like Luca frowned. And just lately, as Ella grew more and more adventurous now she was finally walking, she often gave Bronte a look of gleaming satisfaction that was Luca through and through.

Ever since she had realised she had left her phone behind Bronte had berated herself. Why hadn't she noticed the clasp on her purse was faulty? She should never have agreed to see him. What was she thinking? What good could come of it? It was perfectly clear he was after a quick affair. She had seen the intention in his dark, smouldering eyes. He wanted her. And that kiss! What had she been doing, responding to him like that? What madness had overtaken her? He was testing the waters and they were as hot as he had arrogantly expected.

Fool, fool, fool! Why had she fallen for it? She should have been more determined, more strident, more…more…in control of herself.

She rested her hot forehead on the wall of the lift, trying to get her breathing to calm down. All she had to do was pick up her phone and leave. Simple. Just take it and leave. Don't talk, don't linger and for God's sake don't look at him too long in case he saw more than she wanted him to see.

The lift seemed to take ages to climb to the penthouse floor, or perhaps that was because Bronte was sweating out each heart-stopping second in a rising state of panic.

Finally the lift arrived and she walked on legs that felt as spindly and unstable as a newborn colt's. Her brief knock on Luca's door was answered by him after an annoyingly lengthy interval. She wondered if it had been deliberate.

'Come in,' he said, holding the door wide open.

'No, thank you,' she said tightly. 'I'll just take my phone and leave.'

He folded his arms across his broad chest, rocking back on his heels in an indolent manner. 'Since you've driven all this way back here, why not stay a while and chat?'

Bronte held out her hand. 'My phone.'

Luca took her hand and tugged her into the suite, closing the door with a sharp click behind her. He smiled mockingly at her shocked and outraged expression. 'My way, Bronte, or you won't get your phone back at all.'

She glared at him with eyes as narrow as that of an embroidery needle. 'That's theft, you bastard.'

'You can have your phone after we've had a little talk,' he said, leading her into the suite.

She tugged at his hold to no avail. 'I don't want to talk to you, Luca.'

'Would you like a drink?' he asked, pointedly ignoring her attempts to pull away. 'I'm afraid there's not much champagne left. But I could always open another bottle.'

'I am not here to socialise,' she said through clenched teeth. 'I just want to get my phone and go home.'

He held her in front of him, looking down at her flushed features and tightly pursed lips. 'Why didn't you tell me about your child?' he asked. 'I'm assuming it's yours? She looks the image of you.'

Her face paled and her eyes looked stricken. 'You looked at my photos?' she asked in a hoarse-sounding whisper.

'There was nothing too incriminating there, I can assure you,' Luca said. 'No boudoir scenes, for instance.'

Her face regained some of its colour, two hot spots on each cheek. 'You had no right to touch my phone.'

'On the contrary, Bronte, it was on my sofa and it rang while I was holding it,' he said. 'Did you want me to ignore your call?'

She gave him an icy glare. 'That's what you would have done in the past, wasn't it?'

Luca had to admit she had won that round. He could hardly tell her now how hard it had been to see his phone ringing with her number showing on the screen and having to restrain himself from picking it up just to hear her voice one more time. In the end he had changed phones and numbers so in a weak moment he would not be tempted. And there had been many weak moments over the following months. 'How seriously involved are you with the father of your child?' he asked. 'You're not wearing a wedding ring so I am assuming you're not married.'

She looked at him for a long moment, her eyes flickering with something he couldn't quite identify. Her teeth caught at her bottom lip, pulling at it until he was sure she was going to draw blood. 'No, I'm not married...I... The thing is...' She winced as if she found the subject painful to talk about.

'You're no longer together, is that it?' he said.

She gave her lip another gnaw and finally released it. 'Yes...something like that...'

'Well, then,' Luca said. 'At least we've cleared

up that little detail. There is a lot I would do to get you back into my bed, but taking on a jealous husband is not one of them.'

'I am not going to—'

Luca put a finger against her lips. 'Don't speak so soon, *cara*,' he warned.

Her eyes flared as he brushed his finger along her lips. The softness of her mouth had always amazed him. She had a classically bee-stung mouth, irresistibly kissable. He bent his head and gently brushed his mouth over her lips, tasting her sweetness, wanting more, but holding back to give her time to reveal how much he affected her. Her lashes came down over her eyes, her tongue darting out and depositing a light sheen of moisture over her lips before disappearing again. He felt her breathe, in and out, a ragged sort of sound that seemed to catch inside her chest.

He bent his head again, hesitating just above her mouth, waiting for her to meet him halfway. 'Go on, *cara*,' he whispered against her lips. 'You know you want to.'

'I don't want to…' Her eyes met his briefly

before falling away again. 'I don't want to see you. I don't think this is a good idea…you know…rehashing the past. It never works.'

He brought up her chin again, holding her gaze with his. 'We could make it work. Just you and me. No one else needs to know.'

She pushed against his chest and slipped out of his hold, crossing her arms over her body, turning away from him. 'There's not just the two of us to consider any more,' she said. 'I have a child. I have to consider her. She is my first priority. She will always be my first priority.'

Luca raked a hand through his hair. He didn't want to think about her love-child. It wasn't that he didn't love kids; he did and had always hoped he would have a family of his own one day. He just couldn't get used to the idea of Bronte being a mother to someone else's baby.

Had she had the child as a result of a rebound affair? That somehow made it so much worse. If things had been different, he would have loved to have married Bronte and had the family he knew she wanted. She had hinted at it once or twice but he had deliberately avoided picking up the bait. It had been too painful back then to think about the life he wanted and the life he had been given. The bond of a child was a big deal. What if she still felt something for this guy? The kid was adorable. How could Bronte not feel something for the father of her little baby girl?

Luca had a bigger fight on his hands than he had thought. If he was to somehow convince her to get involved with him again he would have to learn how to be a stepparent. And it was not the easiest of relationships either. He had several friends who had never got on with their parents' partners. It had caused numerous arguments and resentments, some of which went on over years. Bronte's little girl was very young, but nothing could change the fact that Luca was not her real father. Circumstances had prevented him from having that privilege and there was nothing that he could do to change that now.

'How old is she?' he asked.

Bronte pushed a strand of hair back behind her ear and almost but not quite met his gaze.

'She recently turned one.' *Recently, as in two months ago,* she silently added.

His forehead creased as he did the numbers in his head. 'So you hooked up with her father what…a couple of months after you came back to Melbourne?'

Bronte hated lying outright but what else could she do? She hadn't had time to think this through. Everything had happened so quickly. Luca suddenly turning up at the studio—was it only that afternoon? And this evening's awkward meeting and the careless loss of her phone had not given her time to get her head around everything. 'Is that so wrong?' she asked, taking an evasive approach. 'You would have moved on just as, if not more quickly.'

'But to get pregnant to some guy you hardly knew—'

'Don't preach at me, Luca,' Bronte said in irritation. 'I did know him. I thought I knew him well. It just didn't work out.'

'Do you still see him?' he asked. 'Does he have contact with the child?'

Bronte realised now how many lies it took

after you told one to keep the others in place. There was going to be no way out of this other than more and more lies. She hated herself at that moment. It seemed so wrong to lie to him and yet the alternative was too terrifying. Maybe she could work up the courage over time. Maybe there would be a right time to tell him. Maybe they could become friends first and then she could tell him he was Ella's father. Yeah, right, maybe she was kidding herself. She looked at his brooding frown and inwardly gulped. Yep, she was definitely kidding herself. 'No,' she said.

'What? You mean he doesn't want contact with his own flesh and blood?' he asked with an incredulous look.

'Look, Luca, I'd rather not talk about it,' she said. 'If I could just take my phone and—'

'So how do you manage?' Luca asked. 'Does the father contribute financially to the child's upbringing?'

The child. How impersonal he made it sound, Bronte thought. 'Her name is Ella,' she said.

'And I manage perfectly fine without help from anyone.'

'How do you work and look after a little child?' he asked, still frowning darkly.

'The same way thousands of other working single mums do,' she said, 'juggling, compromise and guilt.'

'So that's why you live with your mother.'

'Yes,' she said. 'It works out for both of us. She works part-time and I work on her days off so she can mind Ella.'

He continued to look at her with a frown pulling at his forehead. His hands were thrust in his trouser pockets, the sound of his change and keys rattling the only sound breaking the heavy silence.

'I really should get going,' Bronte said. 'Mum stays in the granny flat with Ella. She can't go to bed back at her house until I get home.'

'If I hadn't ended things with you the way I did, do you think you would be in this situation now?' Luca asked, looking at her intently.

Bronte felt the pull of his magnetic gaze, her heart stumbling like a long-legged horse stepping into a deep pothole. 'There's no point in discussing it,' she said. 'Life happens. It's not as planned as we would like to think it is.'

'Did you plan to get pregnant?'

'No, that was an accident,' she said. 'But it's not one I regret. Ella's the best thing that's ever happened to me.'

Luca took the phone out of his pocket and handed it to her. 'I guess you will need this,' he said. 'She's very cute by the way. She looks exactly like you.'

Bronte felt a thick lump lodge in her throat. 'Th…thank you.' She clutched the phone to her thumping chest, blinking back tears of relief, regret and deep self-loathing.

He stepped closer and cupped her cheek, holding her face so tenderly more tears came to her eyes. 'Why are you crying, *cara*?' he said softly.

She swallowed and gulped back a sob. 'It could have been so different…' She blinked a couple of times but the tears still fell. 'I wanted it to be so different…but now it's too late…'

He brought her head against his chest, his

fingers splayed in her hair, the deep rumble of his voice as he spoke tearing Bronte's heart in two. 'I know, but that is my fault, *mio piccolo*. I wasn't ready. I was in a bad place in my life. I wasn't able to give you what you wanted. But then I wasn't even able to give myself what I wanted. It was just not our time.'

Bronte stood in the circle of his arms, wishing she could stay there for ever. But after a moment he stepped back from her. His expression was hard to read. He was smiling but it wasn't a smile that reached anywhere near his eyes. There were shadows there instead, flickering shadows that gave no hint of what he was feeling.

'I should let you get home to your little girl,' he said, sliding his hands down her arms to her wrists, holding them loosely with his long fingers.

A pain deep inside her chest made it almost impossible for Bronte to speak. 'It was…it was nice to see you again, Luca.'

He brought one of her hands up to his mouth, pressing his lips to her bent fingers. 'I hope one day you will forgive me for how I ended things,' he said.

'It's OK,' Bronte said. 'I should have accepted your decision. I think I made a terrible fool of myself. Actually, I *know* I made a terrible fool of myself. I practically stalked you. I was so desperate to tell you I was…' She stopped and quickly regrouped. 'I mean…I was so desperate to know if there was something I had done to upset you. I should have realised our relationship had run its course. You had never offered anything permanent and I was a fool to hope and dream you would. I was caught up in the whole romance of my first real love affair. I was too immature to see it. Perhaps I didn't want to see it.'

'Don't beat yourself up about it, Bronte,' he said. 'We have this chance now to see if we can make a better go of it.'

Bronte felt her heart give a flutter like a startled pigeon. 'Y-you want to… I mean you still want to… I can't, Luca. I can't see you. I told you that.'

His jaw took on an uncompromising set. 'You

told me yourself there is no one else in your life. What's to stop us revisiting our relationship if it's what we both want?'

'It's what you want,' she said. 'It's not what I want at all.'

'I don't believe that,' he said, tightening his hold on her wrists as she tried to get away. 'The way you kissed me earlier told me how much you still want me.'

'You made me kiss you,' she argued.

'Don't split hairs, Bronte,' he said. 'We were kissing each other. We want each other just as much as we ever did.'

'I can't have a casual affair with you,' she said. 'I have responsibilities now. I haven't got room in my life for you.'

'Make room,' he said and, tugging her close, brought his mouth down on hers.

CHAPTER FIVE

'Gosh, you look like you didn't get any sleep at all last night,' Rachel said as Bronte came into the studio the next day. 'Was it your hot date or your darling daughter who kept you up all hours?'

Bronte gave her a don't-speak-to-me-about-it look.

'Come on, Bronte,' Rachel pleaded. 'You didn't even return any of my texts. What happened? Did you tell him about Ella?'

Bronte blew out a sigh. 'No, I didn't get around to it.'

Rachel's brows went up. 'What *did* you get around to?' She leaned closer and peered at Bronte's chin. 'Hey, is that what I think it is?'

Bronte put her hand up to the reddened patch on her chin where Luca's evening stubble had left its mark. 'It's nothing,' she said.

Rachel folded her arms in a you-can't-fool-me pose. 'Beard rash only happens when you get up close and personal,' she said. 'So the spark is still there, huh?'

Bronte pulled her hair back into a high ponytail, all the while trying to avoid her friend's eyes. She felt so conflicted about last night. That final kiss had burned her like fire. The stubble rash on her chin was nothing to what she felt inside. She was still smouldering with want, a hot needy craving for more of Luca's touch. He had ended the kiss and sent her on her way, only after he had extracted a promise to meet him for dinner this evening. She had practically stumbled back to her car, her emotions on a roller coaster ride as she thought of the danger she was dancing with.

She had spent most of the night once she got home arguing with herself over whether she should have told him from the get-go about Ella. But then the counter argument was always the same: how could she trust him not to take Ella away from her? After all, he had left her in London without a single explanation as to why their affair was over. What was to stop him doing the same thing again, but this time taking Ella with him? It was just too risky. She had to protect her daughter. She had to protect herself.

'So are you seeing him again?' Rachel asked.

'Yes,' Bronte said, slipping out of her street shoes to begin her stretches. 'Dinner tonight. I don't know why I agreed to it. I know it's only asking for trouble. He wants to resume our relationship as if nothing happened.'

'That's men for you,' Rachel said, rolling her eyes. 'So did he tell you why he broke things off before?'

'Not really,' Bronte said, frowning. 'Just that it was a bad time for him or something.'

'You think there was someone else?'

Bronte let out another long breath. 'I don't know what to think. When I spoke to the housekeeper at his place in Milan she was adamant he was involved with someone in LA.'

'But?'

Bronte met her friend's grey gaze. 'I get the feeling Luca is not being totally straight with me. I don't trust him. I don't think I will ever trust him after what he did. He could have a woman in every country for all I know.'

'You said he wants to resume his relationship with you,' Rachel said. 'But how are you going to do that without telling him about Ella?'

'He knows about Ella,' Bronte said. 'He just doesn't know she's his. I left my phone behind and he saw some of the pictures I'd taken of her lately. I let him assume she was someone else's child.'

Rachel frowned. 'How'd you do that?'

Bronte gave her a sheepish look. 'I sort of lied about her age.'

Rachel shook her head in disapproval. 'That could come back to bite you, Bronte. You should have told him. It will only make things much worse the longer you leave it.'

'I can't tell him,' Bronte said, pressing a hand to her aching head. 'He could take her off me. You don't know what the Sabbatinis are like, Rachel. They're one of the most powerful dynasties, not just in Italy but all over Europe. They're practically royalty. They have money and prestige and power beyond belief. I spent a bit of time on the Net last night when I couldn't sleep, looking them up. His father died about three years before I met Luca, but Giancarlo and Giovanna Sabbatini brought their three sons up with more silver spoons than you could possibly count. Luca's grandfather, Salvatore, is reputed to be one of the richest men in the whole of Europe. Luca told me very little of his background when we were involved. I'm not sure why, maybe because so many women were attracted to him and his brothers because of their wealth. I didn't even know who he was when we met. He thought that was highly amusing. I think it might have been one of the reasons he let our relationship continue as long as it did as it was such a refreshing change from what he was used to. He was sick of people fawning over him. He once said to me it is hard to really know who your friends are when you have money.'

'You do realise that Ella is by birth entitled to some of that money, don't you?' Rachel said. 'She's got Sabbatini blood in her veins.

And, according to what I read in the papers about Luca's older brother's marriage breaking up without an heir, Ella is so far the only grandchild.'

Bronte pressed her lips together. She hadn't thought of it quite like that. She hadn't thought about Ella's rights and entitlements as a Sabbatini heir. What if some time in the future her daughter resented her for not allowing her to get to know her father and his family?

'Look, Bronte,' Rachel went on. 'I know Luca hurt you and you don't trust him not to hurt you again, but you can't keep his own flesh and blood a secret from him for ever. For all you know, he might be surprisingly good about it. After all, he was the one who cut you from his life. You did your best to contact him so if anyone's to blame for him not being a part of Ella's first year and a bit, it's him.'

Bronte's shoulders sagged. 'I know I have to tell him some time. It's just finding the right time to do it.'

'There's probably never going to be a perfect time to drop that sort of news into the conversation,' Rachel said. 'But it's better he hears it from you rather than from someone else or, worse, stumbles across the truth himself. Photos are not the same as seeing someone face to face. As soon as Luca walked in here yesterday I realised who he was. That's why I kept my mouth shut. Ella might favour you primarily, but no one could ever question she wasn't his daughter. Once he sees her in the flesh, he's going to see it for himself.'

Bronte tried to put her fears aside as she got on with her day but it was impossible to ignore the prospect of the evening ahead. She got home early enough to feed Ella her dinner and bathe her and have some play time before putting her to bed. Ella was a little grizzly and out of sorts and kept gnawing on her fingers, which made Bronte feel uneasy about leaving her.

'I think she might be teething again,' Bronte's mother said as she came into the granny flat to babysit. 'She was a bit grumpy yesterday too.'

Bronte placed her hand on her daughter's forehead, frowning as she felt its clammy heat. 'I'd better check her temperature. She feels hot.'

Tina produced the rapid test ear thermometer and handed it to Bronte. The reading was normal but still Bronte felt in two minds about leaving her daughter in such an unsettled state. 'Maybe I should ring Luca and cancel,' she said. 'He gave me his contact details. Or I could just leave a message with the concierge at the hotel.'

Tina plucked the whining child from Bronte's arms and cuddled her close. 'Get it over with, love,' she said. 'Have dinner with him and then say goodbye and leave it at that. He'll soon get the message you're not interested. I know Rachel thinks you should tell him about Ella but I think you'd be better to let this particular sleeping dog lie.'

Bronte knew why her mother was so adamant about keeping Ella's paternity a secret from Luca. Tina was frightened her little granddaughter would be taken to live far away in another country. Apart from Bronte and Ella, Tina had very little in her life. A single mother herself from a young age, all she had was her work at a machinery parts factory, which could hardly be called a fulfilling career. Bronte and now little Ella were the entire focus of her life. She had never dated, rarely socialised and had few hobbies. Rachel had warned Bronte many times that her mother was living her life vicariously through Bronte but it had been too hard for Bronte to do anything about it. She had needed her mother, just as much if not more than her mother needed her.

'If she doesn't settle, promise you'll ring me,' Bronte said as she rummaged through her wardrobe for something to wear.

'She'll be fine,' Tina assured her. 'I'll nurse her for a while until she drops off.' She looked down at the infant in her arms and continued wistfully, 'I love watching her sleep. It reminds me of when you were a baby. It was just you and me in those days. I don't know what I would have done if anything had happened to you. You were my whole world.'

Bronte smiled and leant down to kiss her mother and her little daughter. 'I won't be late,' she said softly. 'And thanks, Mum, for everything.'

Tina smiled back but Bronte could see there was a tinge of worry in her eyes as she watched her leave.

Luca straightened his tie and shook down his shirt cuffs, freeing them of his dinner jacket. He had had meetings all day and his head was buzzing with all the things he had to do over the next month. This trip to Melbourne was proving to be one of the best decisions of his career in the family corporation. He had begun the negotiation for plans for a boutique hotel development in the city as well as two more commercial property investments: a large office block in the CBD and a parking lot with the potential for expansion.

And then there was Bronte. He had found it hard to sleep last night once she had left. He still couldn't believe he had let her leave. He had been so close to pulling her back towards his bed and solving the issues over the past by doing what they had always done best. The trouble was he wanted her to come to him willingly. Seduction was easy; working on a relationship was harder. He didn't want to end up like his brother Giorgio with a bitter estrangement from his wife and very likely a costly and acrimonious divorce pending. Luca wanted to get it right this time. He wanted to start again, put the past aside and work on his future—the future he hadn't been sure he would have. Life for him now was about living. Taking each day as a blessing and moving forward with renewed purpose. Bronte was his stumbling block to moving on. He had to know if he had a chance to make things right with her. To see if what they'd had was still there.

The issue of her child was something he found challenging but it wasn't the child's fault and he knew he would learn to love her as his own once he spent some time with her. His family might not see it quite that way but he would deal with them if and when the time came. The pressure for the acquisition of a Sabbatini heir had already caused the breakdown of his brother's marriage. Giorgio and Maya, in spite of several gruelling IVF attempts, had failed to produce the grandchild and great-grandchild his mother and rapidly ageing grandfather longed for.

There was a tentative knock at the door and Luca gave his hair one last finger-comb before he went to answer it. He had wanted to pick Bronte up but she had insisted on meeting him here. The restaurant was only a short walk along the Southbank complex so he had agreed, knowing that pressuring her too much would only bring her back up. It wasn't his intention to antagonise her. His intention was to get her back into his life and into his bed as quickly as possible, to reawaken the feelings he hoped she still had for him. It was a gamble but he couldn't rest until he knew for sure. He saw the way her eyes flared when they met his, and the way she sent the tip of her tongue out over her lips as if anticipating his next kiss. He felt the tension in the air, the way the invisible current of energy drew them together, as it had always done in the past. She might have slept with another man since, but he felt sure she still wanted him.

He opened the door and she was standing there

in a cocktail dress of an intriguing shade of blue. The colour made the dark blue of her eyes look like fathomless lakes. She smelt divine: a mixture of orange blossom and ginger this time, spicy and fragrant and intensely alluring. Her straight dark brown hair was loose about her shoulders, glossy as silk, held back from her face with a slim black headband. Teamed with the cocktail dress, it gave her a child-woman look that was amazingly sexy. She was wearing heels but she still had to crane her neck to meet his eyes. Her mouth was soft and shiny with lipgloss, but in those first few moments he noticed how her teeth nibbled at the inside of her mouth, as if she was nervous.

'Bronte,' he said, leading her into the suite. 'How do you manage to always look so beautiful and elegant?'

She gave him a tentative smile but it was so fleeting he wondered if he had imagined it. 'I picked this up at a second-hand clothing store. At ten dollars it was a steal. I don't have too many fancy clothes.'

Luca wondered if she was deliberately

reminding him of the different worlds they lived in. He had always found it amazing how money had never impressed her. She found pleasure in the simplest things. He had learned a lot from the short time he had been with her. He had learned that money could bring comfort to your life and privileges but it didn't necessarily bring happiness and fulfilment and it certainly didn't guarantee good health.

He led the way to the lounge area and, once she was seated, he handed her a gift-wrapped package.

She looked up at him with rounded eyes. 'What is this for?'

'Open it,' he said. 'I thought after last night it might come in useful.'

She unpeeled the satin ribbon tied around the package and then carefully peeled back the layers of tissue to reveal the designer clutch purse he had bought in between meetings earlier that day. He watched as she ran her index finger over the designer emblem, before lifting her gaze to his. 'It's beautiful...thank you...but you shouldn't have spent so much money.'

'You'd better check to see if the catch works,' he said with a wry smile.

She bit down on her lip and she opened and closed the purse with a snap that sounded like a gunshot. He saw her slim throat rise and fall over a tight swallow and the way her fingers trembled slightly as she refolded the tissue around the purse. A small frown had lined her smooth forehead and when she looked up at him again he saw a shadow of uncertainty in her eyes. 'Luca…' She moistened her lips and started again. 'There's something we need to discuss…I should have told you last night but there didn't seem to be—'

Luca moved to where she was sitting and placed his hand on her shoulder. 'If you're going to make a fuss about me buying you things, then don't,' he said. 'I know you can't be bought with money. I shouldn't have pulled that stunt over the rent. I admire your independence. But this time just accept this in the spirit in which it is given.'

She rolled her lips together and looked down

at the purse lying on her lap. 'It's very kind of you. I really needed a new purse. Thank you.'

He held out a hand. 'Come on,' he said. 'Let's get going to the restaurant. I made an early booking as I figured you would probably need to get home at a reasonable hour to your little girl.'

Her eyes darted away from his. 'Yes…yes, I will.'

Luca took her hand as they walked down to the restaurant. Her small fingers interlaced with his, but he sensed tension in them, a fluttering nervousness that made him wonder if she was having second thoughts about this evening. He had told her no strings, just dinner, but the pulse of electricity that already charged between their bodies was a heady reminder of all they had experienced together in the past. Was she thinking of how many times dinner together had led to mind-blowing sex soon after? His body twitched in memory, his blood surging to his groin as he walked his mind back through the images he had stored of them together. He had clung to those memories during his darkest hours. They had been a powerful motivation for him to fight his demons, to wrestle them to the ground so he could finally reclaim his life.

The restaurant overlooked the Yarra River and the city beyond. There were clouds in the night sky, brooding clusters of tension that crackled in the eerily still air.

'Do you think there is going to be a storm?' Luca asked, pointing to a particularly furious-looking cloud bank in the distance. 'It certainly feels like it, don't you think?'

'I heard something about it in the weather report in the taxi,' she said.

Luca stopped to frown down at her. 'I thought you were going to drive in. I would have picked you up. Why didn't you call me and tell me you'd changed your mind?'

She turned her gaze to the grumbling clouds. 'I was running late. Ella was a bit unsettled. I wasn't sure I'd find a parking spot.'

Luca waited until they had resumed walking before he asked, 'Is that why you're so tense this evening? Are you worried about being away from her?'

'It's hard not to worry at times,' she said, not looking his way, nor at the view but at the ground at her feet. 'It's part of being a parent. You never stop worrying from the moment they are born.'

'I guess you're right,' Luca said. 'My brothers and I are all in our thirties but my mother is always worrying about something or other to do with one or all of us. Mind you, I think there have been times when she has had good cause to be worried. The three of us have had our fair share of mishaps, and then, of course, there was the death of our sister when she was a baby that really did the damage.'

Bronte stopped in her tracks and looked up at him in shock. 'You never told me you had a sister.'

He gave a shrug. 'It was a long time ago. I hardly even remember her, or only vaguely. She died when I was three and Nic was eighteen months old. He doesn't remember her at all. Giorgio remembers her the most clearly. He was six at the time. It really affected him. He won't talk about it, even after all these years.'

'What happened?' Bronte asked.

'Sudden Infant Death Syndrome,' he said. 'Or cot death, as it was called back then. My parents went through a terrible time, my mother especially. There wasn't the knowledge about the cause of it then. My mother felt everyone blamed her. The truth is, she blamed herself. The police who came to the villa after Chiara died didn't help matters. It was a long time before my mother got over it, although, at times, I wonder if she really ever did get over it. She's completely obsessed about having grandchildren, my grandfather too, especially after my father died. It's made things extremely difficult for Giorgio and his wife. I am sure it's one of the reasons they have separated. Maya couldn't take the pressure of not being able to conceive.'

Bronte felt a hammer blow of guilt assail her. She even stumbled slightly, as if the blow was physical. Luca's hand tightened on hers as he steadied her, his brow creasing as he looked down at her.

'Careful,' he said. 'I don't want you to break an ankle on our first date.'

She gave him a strained smile and continued walking. 'I'm sorry about your family's loss,' she said after a moment. 'I'm sorry too about your brother and his wife. It must be a very difficult time for both of them.'

'It is,' Luca said. 'As much as I'd like to knock both their heads together at what they are throwing away, I've had to stay out of it. Giorgio can be very stubborn and once his mind is made up, that's it. He's too proud for his own good. But then, who I am to criticize?'

Bronte mulled over that while he led her into the restaurant. It was a while before they were alone again. The waiter brought drinks and discussed the menu and the day's specials and then reappeared with warmed olives and freshly baked bread and a tiny dish of extra virgin olive oil and balsamic vinegar, before discreetly moving away to leave them in their intimate corner.

Luca raised his glass to Bronte. 'Here's to new beginnings.'

Bronte's hand shook as she touched her glass against his. 'To...to new beginnings.'

The silence fell like a thick suffocating blanket.

Bronte could barely breathe as each second passed. The restaurant noise of dishes and cutlery and glassware faded and her ears filled with a roaring sound of impending doom. Outside, a loud crack of thunder sounded, making her flinch and almost spill her glass of wine.

'Hey.' Luca took her free hand and gave it a gentle squeeze. 'Are you OK? Is the storm bothering you? Are you frightened of them?'

Bronte shook her head. 'No, not really.'

He studied her for a moment. 'You seem really on edge, *cara*. You don't need to be. Just relax. We're just two friends having dinner, remember? I'm not going to put the hard word on you at the end of the evening. We can take things as they go. No pressure, OK?'

Bronte felt sick with nerves. There was no easy way to say what she had to say. She had only made things worse by leaving it this late. She should have told him as soon as he saw the photos of Ella. Why had she made it so hard for herself by dragging it out so torturously? She took a large sip of wine to garner her flagging courage. The crisp dry wine moistened her dry throat but the shot of alcohol did nothing to settle her frazzled and frayed nerves. 'Luca,' she began, 'I have something to tell you.'

'Don't say you don't want to see me again,' he said before she could continue. 'We both know that is not the case. I know I stuffed things up before but I want to make it up to you. I think we have something special, Bronte. I think it could work if we just give it a try.'

Bronte toyed with the stem of her wine glass. 'Are you saying you…you have feelings for me?'

His small smile was enigmatic. 'You wouldn't be sitting here with me now if I didn't feel something. As to exactly what it is, well, isn't it a bit early to be talking about that?'

She ran her finger around the base of her glass this time, her eyes falling away from his. 'I'm not sure how to tell you this, Luca. I never thought I would be in this situation.' Her heart felt as if it was weighted. It ached with a bittersweet pain that made her want to break down and cry for how unfair life was. She had longed for him to give her some clue of his feelings in the past and yet, now he had, she was about to destroy them, she was sure.

She looked up and met his gaze across the table. 'When you left me in London I was devastated. I know you never promised me anything. I know I was much more in love with you than you were ever going to be with me. You never said what you felt. I know a lot of men are like that. Most of my friends experienced the same frustration of never knowing what the man they were dating felt about them. To be frank, sometimes I thought you didn't even like me, that you were just there for the sex. You seemed to give me so many mixed signals. We were all set for a date and then you would suddenly cancel half an hour before. And then you were grumpy and difficult one day and yet charming and attentive the next. I never knew where I stood with you, but I tried to be patient because I loved you so much.'

Luca reached for her hand again, lacing his fingers with hers. 'Back then, I wasn't in the position to offer you the sort of commitment you wanted, Bronte. I know that's not much of an explanation but I'd rather not go into the reasons why I acted the way I did. It's not relevant to here and now. All that matters is we are together again and both committed to working at what we had before. We've been given a second chance. Let's not blow it. Let's work on getting to know who we each are now, not who we were back then.'

Bronte looked down at their joined hands and let a few more seconds thrum pass. It was like waiting for a bomb to go off, watching the timer countdown second by agonising second and being able to do nothing to stop it. She knew once she said the words nothing would ever be the same. She slowly raised her eyes to his, her aching throat going up and down over a convulsive swallow.

'Bronte!' A female voice spoke from behind her in the restaurant.

Bronte pulled her hand out of Luca's and turned in her seat as one of the young mothers from the studio approached the table, her husband in tow. It took Bronte a moment to gather herself and she worried that her smile might not have seemed wholly genuine. 'Hi, Judy...hi, Dan.'

Judy waggled her brows expressively as she glanced at Luca before returning her gaze to Bronte's. 'So...who's your date?'

'Um...sorry,' Bronte said. 'Judy, Dan, this is Luca Sabbatini. Luca, Judy and Dan's daughter Matilda does ballet at the studio.'

Luca rose and politely shook the couple's hands. 'I'm delighted to meet you both,' he said, smiling that killer smile.

Bronte saw the way Judy's knees practically buckled. 'Lovely to meet you, Luca,' Judy said. 'Wow, Bronte's been keeping you a big secret. How long have you known her?'

'We met a couple of years ago in London,' Luca said.

'You're here for work, aren't you?' Judy's husband Dan asked. 'I'm an architect. The firm I work for are bidding for the contract for your hotel development.'

'Give me your business card,' Luca said, reaching into his jacket pocket for one of his own and handing it to Dan. 'I would be happy to look over your proposal with you. I have a temporary office in the city. My secretary will tee up a time for you to come in and have a chat.'

'That's very good of you, Luca,' Dan said, beaming.

'Does your daughter enjoy her ballet dancing?' Luca asked after a tiny silence.

'Oh, yes,' Judy gushed. 'She's mad about it, has been since she was Ruby's age. That's our other daughter, the baby. Well, not so much a baby now but we always call her that. They seem to grow up so fast. She's the same age as Ella. That's how Bronte and I met. It was in hospital having our babies, wasn't it, Bronte?'

Bronte nodded, barely able to get her voice to work. 'Um…yes.'

Judy prattled on, 'Ella and Ruby have the same birthday. They were born at exactly the same hour. Isn't that the most amazing coincidence?'

There was a split second as Bronte watched

helplessly as the pin was finally pulled out of the grenade.

Judy said, 'They were both born on the fourth of July last year, Independence Day. And at fourteen months old they are both headstrong and independent, aren't they, Bronte?'

CHAPTER SIX

'Y-YES,' Bronte said lamely. 'They are...'

Judy smiled up at her husband. 'I guess we should get going to our table. It's our anniversary.' She turned back to Bronte and Luca, who hadn't said a word, nor moved a muscle. 'Lovely to meet you, Luca. I hope we'll be seeing more of you.'

'I am very sure you will,' Luca said, shaking both of their hands once more.

'And thanks for that offer,' Dan chipped in. 'That's amazingly generous of you.'

'Not at all.' Luca brushed Dan's thanks aside.

The couple moved on and Luca remained standing.

Bronte was looking down at her place setting, her slim shoulders rolled forward, with her teeth gnawing at her bottom lip.

'We're leaving,' he clipped out, throwing some money down on the table to cover their ordered meal.

She looked up at him with a pinched look. 'But…but people will wonder what's—'

Luca snatched at her hand and pulled her to her feet. 'I don't give a flying you-know-what for what people think,' he bit out savagely. 'I am not going to discuss this in a public restaurant.'

Bronte stumbled out of the restaurant with him, desperately hoping Judy and Dan wouldn't notice from their seats towards the back of the room. The tension in Luca's hand as he held hers was almost brutal. His fingers were like savage teeth biting into hers as he pulled her along beside him, his mouth set in a hard flat line. His dark eyes were dangerously brooding, his frown equally so. Once they were outside, every step he took pounded the pavement with his fury. The storm that had been brewing earlier was now in full force, as if it had sided with Luca. The flashing lightning and booming thunder mimicked the expression on his face, the electrifying hatred in his gaze zapping her like lightning each time he looked at her.

Bronte ran her tongue over her dry lips. 'Luca...I was trying to tell you when Dan and Judy arrived...'

His hand tightened like a vice as he swung her to face him. 'You were trying to tell me what?' he asked. 'That you deliberately *lied* to me from the moment you saw me yesterday? You told me the child was one year old. I did the calculations and you knew I would, didn't you? That's why you cut a couple of months off so I wouldn't suspect she was mine.'

Bronte hung her head. 'I'm sorry...'

He wrenched her back along the pavement. 'It's a bit late for an apology, damn it. You have a hell of a lot of explaining to do. I am so angry at this moment you should be thanking God we are in a public place. But you just wait until we get back to my hotel. You had better have your excuses handy.'

Each of his words was like a blow to Bronte's chest. She had known he wouldn't take the news well, but to have heard it the way he did had made it so much worse. He was shocked and angry and rightly so. He had missed out on the most precious first months of his child's life. Even though he had refused to see her after he ended their relationship, Bronte knew she'd had a responsibility to tell him, even if it had to have been in a letter addressed to his villa or house in London. He would have got it eventually. But her hurt at his rejection had made her act in a passive aggressive way. She could see it now. How she had secretly relished the fact he didn't know about Ella. It was her little payback for the heartbreak he had caused her. It was an appalling thing to do and she was deeply ashamed.

She couldn't give back what she had stolen from him. Each day of the fourteen months of Ella's life was irreplaceable. Sure, she had photos documenting every little milestone, but how could that compensate for the real thing? Even if he had not wanted a part in his child's life, he should at least have had the right to choose. She had denied him that right and now he was after revenge. She just knew it. Luca Sabbatini was not the sort of man to walk away from something like this with a shrug of his shoulders. He would want her to pay for what she had done and pay dearly.

The lift journey up to Luca's penthouse felt to Bronte as if she was being led to the gallows. As each floor number flashed past, her heart-beat escalated. She felt sick with anguish, guilt and nerves. Her stomach was curdled with the fear he would take Ella away from her. He'd already said how much his mother longed for a grandchild. And what could be more perfect than a little girl to replace the one she had lost in babyhood? The odds were stacked against Bronte keeping custody. How could she afford to contest such a case? She earned too much to qualify for legal aid and too little to take on the Sabbatini dynasty. But she was not going to give up without a fight. She would do anything to stop him from taking her little girl away from her.

Absolutely anything.

Luca activated the swipe card and practically frogmarched Bronte into the suite. He shut the door with a bang that reverberated like a cannon boom. 'Why the hell didn't you tell me you were pregnant?' he asked.

She looked at him with stricken features. 'I tried to contact you time and time again but you refused to meet me face to face.'

Luca felt a knife jab of guilt but he pushed it aside to make room for his burgeoning anger. 'How did it happen? You told me you were on the Pill and, in any case, I always used protection.'

'I don't know how it happened,' she said. 'I must have missed a dose or something. And then there was that time when the condom broke.'

Luca remembered that time as if it had happened yesterday. He had been so eager to see her after being away on a business trip. He had barely got the condom on in time and then it had broken. 'When did you find out you were pregnant?'

'A week after you told me our relationship was over.' She bit into her lip again and another flick knife of guilt caught him off guard.

Luca took a breath but it felt as if he was breathing through barbed wire. His throat felt raw and his chest so tight it ached unbearably. He scored his hair with his fingers, not surprised to see how unsteady his hand was. He could feel the tremors of rage rolling through him. Rage and remorse, a juxtaposition of emotions that made it hard for him to think clearly.

He had a child.

A little girl.

Fourteen months old and he had not shared a second of it. He had not seen her growing in Bronte's womb; he had not been at the birth. He knew nothing about the birth, how long the labour was, whether she had given birth naturally or by Caesarean. He didn't know whether she had fed the child herself or given her a bottle. He knew nothing about his daughter: the sound of her voice, the feel of her baby skin, the softness of her hair or the touch of her little hands. How could he ever get that time back? How could he forgive Bronte for stealing it from him? It had already poisoned what he felt for her. He had come back with such hope at resuming their relationship. But now he felt as if he didn't know Bronte at all. She had changed. She was a scheming little thief, and his loathing of what she had done made him want to cut her from his life all over again. But he couldn't because of his little daughter. His heart tightened again at the thought of that little girl in the photos he had seen.

His daughter.

'I wanted to tell you in person,' Bronte said in a small voice. 'But you didn't return my calls or emails. I went to your villa in Milan but I was turned away at the door. Your housekeeper said you were with your mistress in the US.'

Luca felt an avalanche of guilt come down on him. He had made it impossible for her to contact him. He had covered his tracks so well, not even his family had been aware of where he was and what he had been doing. He had spun them the same tale: a whirlwind affair in the States. And it had worked, perhaps rather too well. 'You could have sent a letter,' he said, still not quite ready to take the whole blame.

'Is that how you wanted to hear you had fathered a child?' she asked.

'It would be a damn better way than finding out in a restaurant in front of complete strangers,' he shot back.

She lowered her gaze and did that thing with her bottom lip again. 'I told you, I was about to tell you when they arrived...'

'When?' he asked. 'Between the main course and dessert? How were you going to slip it into the conversation? "By the way, I had your child fourteen months ago; I thought you might like to know now that you're here in Melbourne." For God's sake, Bronte, what the hell were you thinking?'

She looked at up at him with tears shining in her eyes. 'I didn't expect to ever see you again. You made it so clear our relationship was over.'

'So you punished me by keeping my child a secret,' he said. 'Is that it? Is that why you didn't try harder to get the message to me?'

Guilt flooded her cheeks a cherry-red. 'I didn't want any of this to happen...'

'Meaning you never intended for me to find out,' he said heavily. 'Well, I've got news for you, Bronte Bennett. I want my child. You have got one hell of a fight on your hands if you think you're going to keep me away from her.'

Bronte felt a rod of anger straighten her spine. 'You can't take her from me, Luca. I won't allow it. She's my child. I'll fight you until my dying breath.'

'You and whose legal team?' he asked with a malevolent look. 'You do realise who you are up against here, don't you? You haven't got a hope of winning this, Bronte. Not a hope.'

Bronte hated herself for doing it but right at that moment her temper got the better of her. 'First you have to prove she is yours,' she said with a jut of her chin. 'Have you thought about that, Luca? How do you know she isn't another man's child? You only saw me two or three times a week when we were together, sometimes even less. I had plenty of time to play around behind your back.'

His expression went as dark as the thunderous sky outside. His hands went to tight fists, his breath hissing out from between clenched teeth. 'A paternity test will soon sort out that. I will apply for one in the morning. If you don't agree, expect to hear from my lawyer.'

Instead of feeling she had won that round, Bronte felt as if she had lost much more than a few verbal points. She had lost his respect. She could see it in his eyes, the way they had stripped her bare. It was one thing for him to have the freedom to see who he liked when he liked but quite another for her to do the same. She had been his possession, his little plaything on the side, and it would infuriate him to think she had given herself to someone else while involved with him.

'Who was it?' he asked through tight lips. 'Anyone I knew at the time?'

Bronte turned away. 'I don't have to explain myself to you. You certainly gave me no explanation for what you got up to when you weren't with me.'

He grabbed her arm and spun her around to face him, his expression still as menacing as the storm raging outside. 'Who the hell were you seeing?' he asked.

Bronte tugged at his hold, squirming at

the bite of his fingers. 'Stop it, Luca. You're hurting me.'

His hold loosened, but not by much. 'Tell me who you were seeing, damn it.'

She felt tears approaching and fought them back valiantly. 'Tell me who you were with in LA,' she said. 'What was her name? Was it someone famous or someone married so you had to keep it a big secret?'

His eyes flickered for a moment, his mouth pulled so tight it was white-tipped at the corners.

'Was she very beautiful?' Bronte asked, struggling now to keep her voice from cracking. 'Did she love you? Did you love her?'

He dropped his hand from her arm and stepped away. He rubbed the back of his neck as if trying to soothe a knot of tension there. He didn't speak. He just stood in front of the bank of windows and looked at the last of the storm's activity outside. His back was like a fortress, a thick impenetrable wall she had no hope of scaling. In spite of his hostility, she wanted to go to him, to put her arms around his waist, to hold him, to breathe in the aching familiarity of his scent.

'Luca?'

He turned to face her, his expression rigid with determination. 'I want to see her,' he said. 'I want to see my child.'

Bronte took a little step backwards. 'You mean…now?'

'Of course I mean now,' he said, scooping up his car keys from the coffee table.

'But she's asleep,' Bronte said. 'And…and my mother's there and—'

'Then it's time your mother met the father of her grandchild,' he said. 'She's going to have to get used to me being a part of the child's life.'

'"The child",' Bronte said, throwing her hands out wide. 'Can you please use her name? It's Ella.'

'Does she have a middle name?' he asked, his eyes hard and black with contempt as they pinned hers.

Bronte compressed her lips. 'Her full name is Ella Lucia Bennett.'

He blinked and the strong column of his throat

moved up and down over a swallow. 'You named her...for me?'

She let out a small sigh. 'I wanted her to have something of you, even if it turned out she never met you. I felt I owed you that. I felt I owed her that.'

A little muscle in his jaw worked for a long moment. 'I want my name on her birth certificate,' he said. 'I don't suppose it's there?'

She shook her head. 'No, I didn't see the point at the time.'

'Did you tell anyone I was the father?'

'Not until recently,' she answered. 'My mother eventually pried it out of me. Rachel figured it out when you came to the studio yesterday.'

There was a small tense silence.

'I'm starting to think a paternity test is going to be a waste of time,' he said. 'You didn't cheat on me, did you, Bronte?'

She shook her head. 'No. There's been no one but you.'

Luca curled his fingers around his keys until the cold hard metal cut into his palm. He needed time to process everything. His head was still reeling with the knowledge he was a father. He felt as if he had been pummelled all over. He ached with a pain he couldn't describe. It was worse than anything he had ever experienced. He couldn't imagine how he was going to sort out the mess his life had suddenly become. Things were going to get a whole lot more complicated when it came down to the practicalities. He lived between Milan and London. Bronte lived in Melbourne. Thousands of kilometres separated him from his daughter. That was one of the first things that had to change. 'Let's get going,' he said, moving across to hold the door open for her.

'Luca...wouldn't it be better to do this tomorrow when we've both had some time to think about things?' she asked. 'To cool down a bit, think things through in a more rational state of mind?'

'What is there to think about?' he asked. 'I want to see my daughter. I haven't seen her once and she's fourteen months old. I am not prepared to wait another hour, let alone another day.'

She moved past him with her head down, her

expression shadowed with worry. Luca wanted her to be worried. He wanted her to be aware of what she had done. He wanted her to feel something of what he was feeling, how cheated he felt, how completely devastating it felt to have your world turned upside down without warning.

After asking for directions to her home, Luca retreated into a brooding silence. He couldn't hope to keep something as big as this silent for long. The press would very likely get in on the news. He had to call his mother and brothers and his grandfather. He didn't want them to read it in the press rather than hear it from him. And then there were legal things to see to, such as changing his will to make sure Ella was well provided for in the event of his death.

And then, of course, there was the issue of where to go from here with Bronte. He glanced at her, sitting with her head bowed, her eyes on her knotted hands in her lap. A sharp little pang caught him off guard when he thought of her trying to contact him with the news of her pregnancy. He wondered what she must have been feeling, alone and abandoned, far away from her family and friends. He thought too of the audition she'd had her heart set on. A once in a lifetime opportunity she had relinquished in order to have his baby. So many women would have chosen another option but she hadn't. She had soldiered on, giving up her dream to give life to his daughter.

'Tell me about the pregnancy,' he said. 'Were you well throughout?'

She lifted her head to glance at him. 'I was sick a lot in the beginning,' she said softly. 'I lost a lot of weight in the first three months but after that things settled down a bit.'

Luca felt another jab of guilt. 'What about the birth? Did you have someone with you?'

'My mother was with me.'

He gripped the steering wheel tighter, thinking of what he had missed out on. That first glimpse of new life, hearing the miracle of that first spluttering cry. 'Was it a natural birth?' he asked once he got his voice into working order.

'Yes. I think the fact that I was fit and well

helped a lot. I had a relatively short labour. It was painful but I wanted to do things as naturally as possible.'

'Were you able to breastfeed her?'

'Yes, but it took a while to get things established,' she said. 'For something so natural it's harder than you think to get things right. I weaned her a couple of months ago, just before her first birthday.'

Luca let silence build a wall between them. He wasn't quite ready to let her off the hook. He knew he hadn't made things easy for her by being so adamant about ending their relationship, but he still felt she could have tried harder, *should* have tried harder.

The closer he got to Bronte's mother's house, the more nervous he felt. His stomach was a hive of restless activity. It seemed like a flock of sharp-winged insects was inside him trying desperately to find a way out.

He was about to see his baby daughter for the first time. He would be able to touch her, to hold her in his arms, to feel her petite little body nestled up against him.

He already loved her.

That had surprised him. He thought he would have to meet her first, but no, as soon as he knew she was alive he felt something switch on inside him. The urge to protect and provide for her was so strong he couldn't think about anything else. He was determined to give her everything money could buy, to give her the sort of childhood that would give her every opportunity to blossom and grow into a beautiful young lady, well educated, compassionate and ready to take on the world.

'It's the third house on the left,' Bronte said. 'The one without a fence.'

Luca parked in front of the small weatherboard house. As far as he could see, it was neat but in no way luxurious. Humble was probably a more appropriate word. There wasn't much of a garden, just a lawn and a few azaleas and camellias that lined the boundary of the block. The contrast with his family's villa, his childhood homes in Milan and Rome and the holiday villa at Bellagio couldn't be more apparent. He knew for certain there wouldn't be any household staff opening the door as they approached, nor would there be a team of gardeners to tend the block, nor a driver at the ready to run errands.

Bronte's car—he assumed it was hers as it had a baby seat in the back—was parked in the driveway. There was no carport or garage. The car was at least fifteen years old and looked as if it needed new tyres. The thought of his child being ferried about in that accident-waiting-to-happen appalled him but he decided to keep that conversation for another time.

The walk to the back of the block where a small granny flat was situated was conducted in a stiff silence. Luca could feel Bronte's apprehension coming off her in waves. One of the curtains twitched aside and he saw a woman whom he assumed was Bronte's mother staring at him with wide, nervous-looking eyes.

Bronte opened the door and led Luca inside. Her mother came towards them, her expression cold and unfriendly.

'You must be Luca,' she said, pointedly ignoring Luca's proffered hand.

'That is correct,' he said, dropping his hand back by his side.

'Mum…' Bronte gave her mother a pained look. 'Do you mind if—?'

Tina Bennett ignored her daughter and addressed Luca. 'What you did to Bronte was unforgivable. You left her pregnant and alone. She was only twenty-three years old. She had her whole life ahead of her and you ruined it.'

'Mum, please—'

Tina continued her attack undaunted. 'Did you ever think what had become of her after you threw her out of your life? Or did you simply move on to the next floozy, someone who was more your type?'

Luca seemed very tall as he stood looking down at her mother, Bronte thought. He contained himself well. He showed no sign of being angry at the way her mother was speaking to him. 'Mrs Bennett—' he began.

'It's Miss,' Tina snapped. 'Like mother, like daughter, Mr Sabbatini. I too was abandoned by the man I loved when I was carrying her. I have never married. Being a single mother makes it hard to find someone who is prepared to love your child as their own. You can ask Bronte about that. She's had one date, one boring, going nowhere date that was really only a favour for her friend Rachel.'

'Mum,' Bronte spoke with firmness, 'I want to be alone with Luca. There are things we need to discuss in private. Thank you for minding Ella for me.'

Tina tightened her mouth as she gave Luca a mother lion protecting her cub look. 'I won't let you hurt her again,' she said. 'You can be sure of that, Mr Sabbatini. Bronte and Ella are all I've got. I'm not going to stand by and watch some rich, spoilt playboy take either of them away from me.'

'It is not my intention to hurt anyone,' Luca said coolly and calmly. 'I am here to see my daughter. That is my priority at this point. Bronte and I haven't yet got around to discussing where we go from here but, as soon as we do, you will be the first to know.'

Tina looked as if she was about to say something else but, after another pleading look from Bronte, she turned on her heel and left.

CHAPTER SEVEN

LUCA turned his gaze to Bronte's, his expression rueful. 'Something tells me I didn't make such a great first impression.'

'I would have liked to have warned her you were coming,' Bronte said with a note of reproach in her voice.

'Don't talk to me about warnings,' he threw back. 'Yesterday I was a single man with no responsibilities apart from my work. Now I find I am the father of a fourteen-month-old toddler.'

Bronte worked hard at holding his accusing gaze. 'I know this must be a shock. And I'm sorry about Mum but she's just being a mum. She's frightened and uncertain about what happens next.'

'So she should be,' he said with a brooding frown.

Bronte felt a quake of unease rumble through her stomach. 'Wh…what do you mean?' she asked.

His eyes held hers for a tense moment, bitterness, anger and vengefulness all reflected there. 'Look at this place,' he said, waving his hand to encompass the small room and simple furnishings. 'This is not the place where I want any child of mine to be brought up. There isn't even a front fence, for God's sake. What if Ella was to walk out on the road? Have you thought of that?'

Bronte summoned her pride. 'There is nothing wrong with this place,' she said. 'The fence is going up as soon as we can afford it. And, anyway, Ella is only just walking and she is never left alone. Not for a minute.'

'That is not the point,' he argued. 'She deserves much better and I am going to make sure she gets it. Now, please lead me to her. I want to see her.'

Bronte clamped her lips down on her response and silently led him to the small bedroom next to hers. The blue angel night light was on, casting a soft luminous glow over the room. Ella was lying on her back, arms flung either side of her head, her rosebud mouth slightly open, the covers kicked off her tiny body. Bronte gently pulled the covers back up, conscious of Luca standing next to her, his eyes looking down at the sleeping infant.

The only sound in the silence was Ella's soft snuffling breathing.

Luca looked at the angelic face of his child and felt a seismic shift inside his chest. He was totally overcome by emotion. Feelings surged through him, knocking him sideways. He swallowed against the lump in his throat, surprised to feel the burn of tears at the backs of his eyes. He blinked them back and, with a hand that was not quite steady, he reached down and brushed his fingertip across the velvet softness of Ella's tiny cheek. She made a little noise, something between a snuffle and a murmur, as if she were dreaming, before settling back down with a little sigh.

Luca picked up one of her tiny hands. It reminded him of a starfish, the little splay of fingers with their perfect fingernails so small in comparison to his. Her fingers curled around one of his, the tiny dimples on her knuckles appearing as she tightened her hold, as if subconsciously recognising she belonged to him. He could not explain how it felt. It was totally overwhelming. He longed to hold on to this moment, to keep it forever in his memory.

How would it feel as the years went by, holding this little trusting hand in his? Walking her into school for the first day, holding her steady as he taught her to ride a bike, her holding on his arm as he led her one day way off in the future to the man who would one day be her husband? It was too much to absorb all at once. Other men had nine months to prepare for it. He had been cheated of that. He was in catch up mode and it hurt—it hurt so much he could barely breathe.

'You can pick her up if you want to,' Bronte whispered at his side. 'She usually sleeps pretty soundly.'

'Can I?' he asked, looking at Bronte for reassurance.

She gave him a tight little movement of her

lips, her eyes suspiciously moist. 'Of course,' she said, reaching past him to ease back the covers.

Luca wasn't sure how to do it but was too proud to ask for help. He had bounced the occasional friend's baby on his knee but he had never picked up a sleeping baby before. Wasn't there something about their neck you had to be aware of?

'Just gather her underneath her shoulders and knees,' Bronte offered in the silence, as if she had sensed his hesitancy.

'Right...' He did as she said and his little daughter nestled against him as he lifted her out of the cot with another soft murmur.

'There's a chair over here.' Bronte pushed it forward and he sat down, cradling Ella against his chest.

Luca couldn't take his eyes off her. The perfection of her amazed him. She had the most beautiful face, like an angel. She favoured her mother, but now that he had her up close he could see traces of his own mother and even his long-dead baby sister. She smelt so sweet, a combination of talcum powder and baby that was indescribably beautiful. He traced a gentle fingertip over each of her tiny eyebrows and then the up-tilted button nose that was so like Bronte's. Love flowed through him like a torrent. It filled him completely; there wasn't a space inside him that wasn't consumed with love for this child.

'Would you like some time alone with her?' Bronte asked after a long silence.

'It's all right,' Luca said, carefully getting to his feet and carrying Ella back to the cot. He laid her down gently and pulled the covers back over her, tucking them in either side of her. 'I don't want to wake her. She might feel frightened at not knowing who I am if she should suddenly wake up.'

He stood back from the cot and took a steadying breath before turning to Bronte. 'We need to talk.'

She nodded resignedly and led the way out of the room.

The kitchen–living room combined was on the small side but with Luca there it made it shrink to the size of a doll's house. There was nowhere in the room that kept her more than two metres away from him. It was intimidating to say the least. One step from him and a reach with one of those long arms of his and she would be snared. The most bewildering thing was, she wasn't entirely sure she would try to move away if he did reach out and touch her.

Bronte was so moved by watching him with Ella. She hadn't been sure what to expect but seeing the love on his face for his child had made her all the more certain he was not going to walk away from his little daughter. He would want to be an active father. He came from a strongly connected family background, a rich heritage that Ella was entitled to be a part of as a Sabbatini. The only trouble was, where did Bronte fit into it all according to his plans for the future?

'Would you like a cup of tea or something?' she asked to fill the silence.

'No tea,' he said.

She gestured to the one and only sofa. 'Would you like to sit down?'

'No, but you had better do so,' he said ominously.

Bronte sat down on the chain store sofa and pressed her knees against her hands to keep them from trembling. 'Don't take her off me, Luca, please, I beg you,' she said, the words tumbling out of her mouth in an agonised stream. 'I love her so much. I would do anything to make it up to you. I know it was wrong not to try harder to tell you. I realise it now. I couldn't bear it if you...' She couldn't continue as the tears began to fall. She bowed her head and stifled a sob.

'Tears are not going to work with me, Bronte,' he said through tight lips. 'I have lost more than a year of my child's life. Do you have any idea of what that feels like?'

She looked up at him with red-rimmed eyes. 'I know how upset you must be—'

'You don't know the half of it,' he ground out. 'I look at Ella and every day I have missed is like a punch to my guts.'

'I have photos and some home videos to show you—'

'For God's sake, Bronte, a child's life is not

like a movie I've missed when it came to the local cinema,' he said, raking a hand through his hair. 'I can *never* have that time back. I can never tell her when she is older what it was like to see her born. I can never tell her what it felt like to hold my hand over your belly to feel her wriggling in there. I can't tell her when she took her first step or when she first smiled.'

'She's still so young,' Bronte said. 'She won't even remember you weren't a part of her life in the beginning. Children don't really remember anything until they are about three years old. You have plenty of time to make up for what you've lost.'

'And how do you suggest I do that?' he asked. 'Aren't you forgetting something?'

Bronte pressed her lips together. She knew what was coming and took a breath to prepare herself for it.

'You live in Australia,' he said. 'I spend half my time in Italy and the other half in London.'

'I…I know…' Her voice was a thready whisper.

'Which means one of us has to move.'

Her eyes rounded, her mouth going completely dry. 'You'd do that? You'd consider moving here to be closer to Ella?' she asked.

His expression was derisive. 'Not me, Bronte,' he said, 'you.'

'Me?' The word came out like a squeak.

'Of course you,' he said. 'I can't run a corporation the size of mine from this distance. You can teach ballet anywhere.'

Bronte got to her feet in one agitated movement. 'Are you out of your mind? I can't move to Italy or wherever you want me to. I'm building up my career. It's just getting to the stage where I can expand and take on more teachers. And I have my mother and friends here. My support network is very important to me.'

His mouth took on a stubborn line. 'You move or you lose Ella,' he said. 'I am not going to have her travelling back and forth in planes on access visits. I want to be fully involved in her life. I am not prepared to negotiate on this.'

Bronte opened and closed her mouth, trying to think of some way to make him see reason. She couldn't believe his obstinacy. Did he really think she should uproot everything at his bidding? What role was she to play in his life? Was she just to be the mother of his child or was he expecting something more?

'I want my family to meet Ella as soon as possible,' he said. 'And it goes without saying we will have to get married as soon as it can be arranged.'

Bronte stared at him in stupefaction. 'Are you crazy?'

'I am not going to be drawn into an argument about this, Bronte,' he said. 'Ella is a Sabbatini. She has certain rights and privileges as a grandchild and heir. I will have no one refer to her as a love-child. I want her to have my name.'

'She can have your name without you having to marry me,' Bronte said. 'I can have it put on the birth certificate.'

'Bronte, let me make something very clear,' he said with an intractable set to his mouth. 'We have a responsibility towards our child. She needs a mother and a father. The only way to see that she gets what she needs is for us to marry and stay married.'

'But I don't love you any more.' Bronte said it even though she wasn't sure if it was true. She didn't know what she felt towards him. She felt so confused about him. He had barged back into her life and was threatening everything she had clung to for security. The hurt over his rejection was like a wound that had been reopened. It ached deep inside her and she was terrified of being hurt all over again.

'I do not require your love,' he said. 'There are plenty of very successful marriages which exist on mutual respect and common interests. We will start with that and see where it takes us.'

Bronte sent him a defiant glare. 'I hope you're not expecting me to sleep with you because I'm not going to. If I have to marry you, it will be in name only.'

His eyes were like glittering black diamonds as they held hers. 'You are not the one dictating the terms here, Bronte,' he said. 'You will be my wife in every sense of the word.'

Bronte's heart gave a nervous flutter as his implacable statement hit home. She could see the fiery intent in his eyes. He wanted her and he was not going to settle for a sterile hands-off arrangement. The thought of sleeping with him was all the more terrifying because she was sure she would fall in love with him all over again. She couldn't dissociate the intimate act like some of her peers seemed able to do. She felt the emotional connection deeply. In the past she hadn't just loved him with her heart and soul, but her body as well. 'You seem to have it all worked out,' she said, trying to keep the wobble out of her voice.

'It's for the best, Bronte,' he said. 'In time, you will see that. I know it is a lot to ask of you to relocate, but your mother can visit any time she likes. And you can fly back for visits. You will not be under lock and key.'

She turned and paced what little space she had. 'I need some time to think about this,' she said, pressing her hand to her temple where a cluster of tension was gathering.

'There isn't time,' he said. 'We have to get moving on this. We have a wedding to arrange.

I want it to be a proper one, not some hole in the corner affair.'

Bronte swung back to face him. 'I haven't said I will marry you, Luca. Don't rush me. I told you I need some time to think about this.'

He came over to where she was standing, his expression so in control, so commanding, so indomitable, it sent a tremor of unease through her. 'If you say no to our marriage, you are never going to see your daughter again,' he said. 'Have I made myself clear enough?'

Bronte bristled with outrage. 'You bastard,' she said in a snarling hiss. 'You arrogant, cruel, heartless bastard.'

His eyes glinted as they roamed her furious features, his body so close now she could feel the male heat of him. She had nowhere to escape. She was backed up against the wall, her heart going like a jackhammer in her chest as he planted his hands either side of her head, his strongly muscled arms making a cage around her quaking body. She sent the tip of her tongue out over her lips, a rush of unruly desire gushing through her like a flash flood.

His eyes went to her mouth, his lashes lowering in a smouldering manner. She held her breath as he came closer, the soft waft of his breath over the surface of her lips making her heart kick-start in reaction. When he finally touched down on her lips she felt an explosion of desire in her body. It roared like petrol thrown on a fire. Leaping flames of need rose up and consumed her. She opened her mouth to the possessive thrust of his tongue, a hollow pit opening in her stomach as it mated erotically with hers. This was no poignant tender kiss of a revisited relationship. This was a kiss of anger and out of control needs. Bronte tasted Luca's anger and frustration and gave plenty of her own back. She used her teeth on his lower lip, not the tender teasing little nips of the past, but savage wildcat bites that drew blood. He took control of the kiss, pushing her further back against the wall, his aroused body hot, hard and urgent against hers.

It shocked her how much he wanted her.

It shocked her how much she wanted him.

Her body had superseded any counter argument

her mind tried to throw up to resist him. The simple truth was she wanted him to make love to her, to reclaim her body, to imprint it with the potency of his.

His mouth was still locked on hers as his hands lifted her cocktail dress, searching for the slick wet heart of her. He cupped her first through the lacy barrier of her knickers, which were already damp with want. She arched her spine as he pushed the lace aside to slide one finger into her. The sensations rippled through her, making her want more and more of his touch. She whimpered against the crushing heat of his mouth as his hand left her moist heat to unzip his trousers. She blindly assisted him, her fingers stroking along his steely length, delighting in the feel of him so aroused. It was something to cling to, this need he had for her. He might not love her, he might never find it in himself to forgive her for denying him knowledge of his child, but he wanted her with a fervency that secretly thrilled her.

She could have pulled away. She could have stopped things before they went any further but she didn't. She dug her fingers into the tautness of his buttocks and urged him on.

He thrust into her with a deep bone-melting thrust that sent her head thudding against the wall behind her. He set a furious pace but she matched it. It didn't matter that they were still fully clothed; it didn't matter that no one had mentioned protection.

The friction of his thickened body brought her undone within seconds. She had never been able to come without added stimulation before but this time her body shattered into a thousand pieces, the convulsions of her inner core setting off his equally powerful release. She felt the pumping of his body as he emptied himself.

His breathing was still uneven as he stepped back from her and re-zipped his trousers. 'That should never have happened,' he said grimly. 'I hope I didn't hurt you.'

Bronte smoothed down her dress. 'I thought that was your intention—to hurt me as much as possible for keeping Ella a secret from you.'

His expression was contorted with regret. 'Anger is a dangerous emotion when it's out of control,' he said. 'I had no right to take it out on you in such a way. I'm sorry. It won't happen again.'

Bronte felt a little sideswiped by his sudden mood change. She wasn't sure how to deal with her own feelings, let alone his. Her body was still humming with the aftershocks of his love-making. She could still feel his presence inside her even now, the twinge of unused muscles and the damp heat of him reminding her of how much passion simmered between them. Those out of control needs were satiated for now, but how long was that going to last? If she were to marry him and live with him there would be no way of ignoring the sexual tension that crackled like a current of electricity between them. She stepped away from the wall and wasn't quite able to disguise a little wince as her body protested at the movement.

Luca's frown deepened. 'I did hurt you, didn't I?'

Bronte felt her cheeks heat up. 'I'm fine. It's just been a long time…well, you know…'

There was an awkward little silence.

'It's been a long while for me too,' he said, rubbing the back of his neck again.

Bronte looked at him, wondering whether to believe him or not. When she'd met him he had a reputation as a playboy. What he wanted, he got. No woman could resist him. She couldn't quite see him adhering to a celibate lifestyle for longer than a week or two. He was too full of life, too full blooded, too intensely and potently male.

He looked at her with a wry expression. 'You don't believe me, do you?'

'Why should I?' she asked. 'You've told me practically nothing of your life over the past two years. For all I know, you've probably had numerous affairs, one after the other. A long time between lovers for you might mean a couple of days.'

He held her look for a long moment before shifting his gaze. 'It's not been like you think, Bronte. I've had other things going on in my life. There has been no one of any significance for quite some time.'

'How very restrained of you,' she said with an attempt at sarcasm.

He ignored her comment and wandered over to the small bookcase and picked up a photograph of Ella. 'You mentioned you had photos and DVDs of her. I would like to have copies made, if you don't mind.'

'Of course I don't mind,' Bronte said. 'I'll get them together for you. I'll have to bring them to your hotel tomorrow, however. Mum has most of them at her house. There's not much storage space here.'

He turned and looked at her. 'Why do you live here instead of in the main house with your mother?'

'I thought it was important to maintain some element of independence for me and for Ella,' she said. 'My mother—as you saw—is rather protective. She means well but at times she can be quite smothering. I make allowances for her because she's been alone for so long. Living here is a sort of compromise. Mum is close by to help me with Ella but there is enough distance, small as it is, to establish some boundaries.'

'How do you think she will take the news of our marriage?'

'The same way I am taking it,' she answered. 'With a great deal of apprehension.'

Luca came back over to her and ran a fingertip down her cheek. She didn't veer away, but he saw the way her eyes flickered with wariness. Her mouth was swollen from his kisses, puffy and pink and all too tempting to kiss again. 'There is no other way to do this, Bronte,' he said. 'You do realise that, don't you?'

She snatched in a breath that seemed to catch in her throat. 'You're blackmailing me, Luca, can't you see that?'

He steeled his resolve. 'I admit it was not the most polished proposal, but the end justifies the means. I want my child. I want to provide for her. I want her to be a part of my extended family. I want her to embrace her Italian heritage, to learn my language. I can't give her that at a distance and you can't do it on your own.'

'But a loveless marriage…' Her eyes communicated her anguish. 'Ella's just a baby now but it won't be long before she's old enough to see things are not quite right between her parents. No amount of money can compensate for that. Surely you see that?'

Luca placed his hands on her shoulders, holding her gaze with his. 'We will work at our relationship. There is no doubt of the attraction that still exists between us. That is a good enough basis to start from.'

'You're asking me to give up everything,' she said, still with that worried look in her slate-blue eyes. 'I have so much more to lose than you. I will be alone in Italy. I don't speak the language, or at least only a few words here and there. What if your family doesn't take to me? Have you thought of that? I have never met them. They will no doubt be just as angry as you are about Ella being kept a secret all this time.'

Luca dropped his hands from her shoulders. 'It won't be easy. I am the first to admit that. I will do what I can to make things go as smoothly as possible. My family will accept you. I will make sure of that. They will adore Ella and in time may come to adore you too. It will take time. You will have to be patient.'

He put some distance between them before he spoke again. 'I will compensate you handsomely for marrying me. I will have an agreement set up by my financial and legal people. That should help dissolve some of your current doubts.'

Bronte screwed up her forehead in a frown. 'You think you can pay me to be your wife? You think I can be *bought*?'

The look he gave her was cynical. 'One thing I have learned through business is that everyone has a price. I am sure you have one too.'

She glared back at him furiously. 'You think you can afford me?' she asked, not caring if she was goading him too far.

His top lip curled upwards with the same cynicism she saw reflected in his gaze. 'Name your price,' he said.

Bronte threw a figure at him, an astonishingly exorbitant sum that would have made most men flinch in response. Luca's expression was mask-like. It showed no emotion. It was as if they were discussing a business transaction.

'Fine,' he said. 'I will make sure the funds are deposited in your bank account as soon as possible. You will need to give me your banking details, unless you would like me to write you a cheque here and now.'

Bronte scribbled her details down on a piece of paper, a war going on inside her over what she had just done. She had sold herself. Her future was now in his hands. She handed him the note, her eyes not quite able to hold his. 'I will need to give the parents of my students some notice,' she said.

'I am sure your business partner will be able to see to everything,' he said. 'I want us to be in Italy at the end of the month. I want our marriage to be conducted at the family hotel in Milan. That way, all of my relatives can be there. It is too far for my elderly grandfather to travel all the way to Australia.'

Bronte's eyes flew back to his. 'Are you out of your mind? I can't possibly tie up everything here in less than three weeks!'

'I am a busy man, Bronte,' he said. 'I have commitments here that will now have to be put on hold until we get back.'

She frowned again. 'So you're expecting me to follow you back and forth across the globe?'

His eyes challenged her to defy him. 'That is what most loving wives would do, is it not?'

It took Bronte a moment to catch on. 'You…you want me to pretend our marriage is normal?'

'But of course,' he said.

She folded her arms crossly. 'That's out of the question. I won't do it.'

'It is not negotiable, Bronte,' he said. 'I will not be made an object of ridicule the world over for having a wife who hates the sight of me. You will at all times and in all places maintain the guise of a devoted wife.'

Bronte fumed as she stood facing him. 'Is this marriage going to be an exclusive arrangement or are you going to continue with your philandering ways?'

He held her gaze for an interminable pause. 'That, *cara*, will depend entirely on you,' he said. 'Why would I stray if all my needs are being met at home?'

'And what about my needs?' she asked, giving him a glowering look.

He picked up his car keys and made his way to the door before he answered. 'I think I showed you only a few minutes ago how effectively I can meet your needs.' His dark eyes ran over her from head to foot, undressing her, caressing her, tempting her all over again. 'As my wife, Bronte, you will want for nothing.'

He closed the door on his exit and Bronte finally let out the breath she hadn't even realised she had been holding.

You will want for nothing, he had said. But what about what she wanted most of all? No amount of money was going to buy her the love she so desperately craved.

CHAPTER EIGHT

BRONTE decided to take Ella with her to Luca's hotel the next day, not just so he could spend time with his daughter if he happened to be there, but more to protect herself from falling into his arms as she had done last night.

Her body was still quivering with aftershocks, her flesh still tender from where he had possessed her so thoroughly. She felt ashamed of how she had fallen into his arms so quickly. Her actions had cancelled out every word of protest she had made to him about resuming their relationship. It would give him all the more power over her. He had always had the advantage. Wasn't it true that the person who had the most power in a relationship was the one who loved less? By loving Luca in the past, she had become the most at risk of being hurt, and that was exactly what had happened. But this time the risk was much higher because Ella was part of the equation.

As soon as Bronte got out of the car a swarm of paparazzi came towards her, seemingly from nowhere. 'Miss Bennett?' A journalist held a microphone in her face. 'Is it true your daughter is the secret love-child of Luca Sabbatini, the hotel tycoon?'

Bronte tried to stop the cameras flashing in little Ella's face. 'Do you mind?' she snapped. 'Keep away from her.'

Several camera shutters went off like a round of air rifle bullets. Ella started to cry and Bronte opened the back door of the car and fished her out of her seat, holding her close against her chest as she walked into the hotel with the bag containing Ella's baby DVDs and photos banging painfully against her hip.

The press followed like a pack of hungry dogs snapping at her heels. She bolted towards the reception counter and, trying to soothe Ella as well as ignore the camera flashes, she handed the bag over to the concierge. 'Could you please put this aside for Luca Sabbatini?' she asked. 'He's staying in the penthouse.'

The concierge smiled and placed a swipe key in front of her. 'Signor Sabbatini asked for you to be given this. If you give me your keys, I will get the valet parking attendant to take care of your car for you. If there is anything we can do to be of assistance with the little one, please don't hesitate to ask. We have cots and baby food and a babysitting service if you should require it.'

'Er… I'm not staying here,' Bronte said quickly. 'I'm just dropping off the bag with… er… I'm just leaving this for him.' She pointed to the bag perched on the counter.

The concierge gave her an urbane smile. 'Signor Sabbatini expressly asked for you to be given full access to his suite. He is not here at the moment but should be back shortly. He would like for you to wait until he returns.'

Bronte ground her teeth. She had two choices: turn around and put Ella through the drama of facing the press again, or go up to Luca's suite and kill some time until the paparazzi left, hopefully before Luca returned. She let out a breath of resignation and picked up the swipe card and the bag of DVDs and photos. 'Thank you,' she said. 'We'll wait for him.'

The suite was blessedly quiet and Bronte was finally able to settle Ella, who had come close to becoming hysterical over the fuss downstairs. Her little face was bright red and her eyes still streaming, and tiny heart-wrenching hiccups were rattling intermittently in her chest. 'Don't cry, darling,' Bronte said softly, rocking her gently from side to side. 'Shh, it's all right. They've all gone away now.'

But for how long? she wondered. And how on earth had they found out about Ella being Luca's child? Had Luca made some sort of announcement without telling her? It was a frightening thought that this was what she and Ella might have to live with: the constant intrusion of the press which Luca had described previously. How would she ever cope with it? How could she protect Ella? She didn't want her daughter terrified every time they went outside. Was this *really* how celebrities and royalty lived? If so, it was absolutely unbearable.

Ella gave one last little hiccup and laid her head on Bronte's shoulder, her dark lashes falling down over her eyes. Bronte carried her through to Luca's bedroom, her stomach giving a little flutter as her eyes went to the bed that looked the size of a football field. She thought of herself lying there in Luca's arms, not in anger or out of control passion but in mutual longing and need.

And love...

No, she checked herself sternly. You don't love him any more. He killed everything you felt for him by shutting you so ruthlessly and mercilessly out of his life.

But still...

The smell of him was in the room, the musk and hint of citrus that she could not, even after two years, get out of her senses.

She laid Ella gently down on the middle of the bed and placed a bank of pillows either side of her to keep her from falling off. She couldn't help a little flare of her nostrils as she held a spare pillow up to her face, breathing in the scent of Luca, a host of memories flooding her brain.

Not one night, she reminded herself as she tossed the pillow to the floor in a fit of pique. He couldn't even stay with you one full night. How on earth do you think he is going to settle down to being married with a child? He wanted custody and he was going about getting it. Bronte was superfluous. She would be dispensed with as soon as the lust he felt for her died down. He didn't know how to run a relationship. He was too selfish, too closed off, too focused on his career. He didn't know how to make sacrifices for other people. He didn't know how to love.

And yet he seemed to love Ella...

Bronte strode out of the bedroom to get away from her traitorous thoughts but they followed her, just as the paparazzi had done earlier. Click, click, click went the shutters of her brain, bringing up the touching moment when Luca had seen Ella for the first time the night before.

Bronte had always found Luca to be so emotionally distant, but last night she had seen a side to him she had never glimpsed before. He had looked down at the child in his arms, his eyes so full of wonder and amazement that she was his. Bronte had thought she had seen a hint of moisture when he'd turned and faced her, but in a blink it had gone so she didn't know if she had imagined it.

The door of the penthouse suddenly opened and Luca came in carrying a briefcase and a toy shop bag bulging with toys. 'Bronte,' he said, frowning. 'The concierge told me there was a bit of scene with the press outside the hotel. Is Ella all right?'

Bronte folded her arms across her chest. 'She was terrified. It took ages to calm her down. She's sleeping on your bed.'

He put the briefcase and toys down and reached up to loosen his tie. 'I should have warned you,' he said. 'I'm not sure how they found out. I was going to make an announcement once I had informed my family.'

'Have you told your family?'

He shrugged himself out of his jacket and laid it over the back of one of the plush sofas.

'Yes,' he said. 'They were shocked, as you can imagine, but pleased, especially my mother. She can't wait to meet Ella. I have promised to email some photos. Did you bring them with you?'

Bronte gestured to the bag on the floor near the sound system. 'I've brought everything I could find. I even have a lock of her baby hair in a matchbox. I found another one this morning and divided the lock in two. I thought you might like one of your own.'

He picked up the bag and found the matchbox. He set the bag back on the floor and looked at the commonplace box for a moment. Bronte watched as his long tanned fingers opened it, his dark eyes homing in on the tiny curl of silky hair. He touched it and smiled, but there was sadness in it.

She swallowed and moved forward, taking the bag off the floor to ferret out the first album of pictures of Ella. 'I haven't had time to make copies of everything. I thought you might like to have it done professionally or something. This one is of the first few months of her life.'

Luca took the album and sat down on the sofa.

Bronte didn't know what to do with herself. She wasn't sure if she should go and sit beside him or leave him alone to view the photos by himself. 'Um…I think I'll go and check on Ella,' she said and darted out.

When she finally came back in, Luca was sitting with his eyes glued to the huge flat screen TV where he had put in one of the DVDs. The sound of Ella's tinkling laughter as Bronte lifted her high in the air filled the room. The next clip was of Ella having her first swimming lesson at the age of six months. They were tears and screams and then happy splashes as she gradually got used to the water on her face during the mother and baby class.

Luca looked up and pressed the mute button on the remote control. 'I can't find a DVD with Ella as a newborn. Do you have one?' he asked.

Bronte went through the bag, feeling self-conscious about how disorganised this was making her appear. Was he criticising her for being a bad mother? Was he thinking a devoted mother would have everything filed in neat, beautifully scrapbooked albums, or DVD cases in chronological order, not stashed haphazardly in a green shopping bag? No doubt his mother would have her sons' locks of hair in priceless heirloom velvet boxes with the family name inscribed on the outside, not in a run-of-the-mill matchbox. She chewed at her lip as she hunted through the bag, the stretching silence shredding at her already overwrought nerves.

'Can't find it?' he asked.

She sat back on her heels. 'I must have missed it when I gathered the others up from Mum's place.'

'I would like to see it,' he said. 'I will come around and get it tomorrow, that is if you can find it by then.'

Bronte got to her feet and glared at him. 'I know what you are implying, so why don't you come right out and say it?'

He didn't rise from the sofa; instead, he sat back and returned her look with the elevation of one of his midnight-black brows. 'And what would I be implying?' he asked.

She hissed out a breath. 'You think I'm doing a bad job of being Ella's mother. I can see it in your eyes. You think because I haven't got all this stuff organised properly I can't possibly be a good mother to her.'

This time he did rise from where he was sitting. His increase in height made the room shrink, irrespective of its commodious proportions. 'I think you are projecting your own insecurities on to me,' he said. 'You are the one who thinks you are an inadequate mother, not me.'

Bronte felt her back come up at his too close to the truth summation of what she felt a lot of the time. 'You don't know anything about parenting,' she threw back. 'You don't know what it's like trying to earn a living and bring up a baby. You don't know what it's like to be so tired at the end of the day or sick and overwrought and still have to get up half the night, if not all the night, to see to a baby's needs. You live in a cotton wool world, Luca, you always have. You don't even have to make your own bed, for God's sake.'

His mouth tensed as if he was holding back a stinging retort, the silence going on and on and on until the air felt thick and too heavy to breathe.

Bronte wondered if she had revealed a little too much of her struggles and if he would go on to use it against her in a custody battle. She was making things so much worse by losing control of her emotions. Like last night, falling so readily into his arms, demonstrating so conclusively how much she still wanted him. She bit her lip and moved to the other side of the room, staring down at the view below rather than see the light of victory shining in his dark eyes. She needed to get away to garner her self-control. She needed to regroup. Her feelings were getting the better of her. Next thing, she would be on her knees begging him to take her back, marriage or no marriage.

'I admit I have a lot to learn,' Luca said. 'But at least I am willing to do so. A lot of men simply walk away from their responsibilities. But I will not. I want to be involved in every way possible with Ella.'

Bronte spun around. 'Well, why don't you start right here and now?'

He frowned as she stalked towards the door, only stopping long enough to take out her purse from the change bag she had brought for Ella. She practically shoved the bag against his abdomen, her eyes flashing at him in frustration and fury. 'Have the rest of the evening with her,' she said. 'You can feed her and change her and try and settle her when she won't be settled. I will be back in a couple of hours.'

Luca flinched as the door swung shut on her exit. He let out a long breath and sent his hand through his hair. He heard a little whimper coming from his bedroom and went through to see if Ella was waking.

She was sitting up in the middle of his bed, surrounded by pillows, two big fat tears rolling down her cheeks. 'Mummy?' She scrubbed at her blue eyes and looked so forlorn Luca felt his heart tighten to the point of pain. 'Mummy gone?'

'Mummy's gone out for a while, *mio piccolo*,' he said and gently lifted her off the bed. 'But *Papà* is here. *Papà* is always going to be here. You will never be alone, my little one.'

Ella smiled at him through her tears and batted at his face with a dimpled hand. *'Papà.'*

Luca cuddled her close, her little legs wrapping around him like a monkey's. She smelt… actually, she didn't smell so good. He looked at the wet patch on his bed and grimaced as he felt the dampness soaking through her candy-pink leggings to his hands. 'I don't suppose you can give me any hints on this process,' he said wryly as he carried her out to the lounge area where the change bag was. He picked it up with his spare hand and took Ella to the bathroom. He put her on her feet on the floor but, before he could even unzip the bag or remove her leggings, she was off. 'Ella, wait,' he said, missing her by millimetres as she giggled and toddled out, her sodden and loaded nappy seeming to mock him as she went.

Luca went in pursuit and captured her just as she knocked an ornament off one of the coffee tables in her effort to hide beneath it. Thankfully, the ornament just thudded to the carpeted floor without breaking and without hurting her. 'You little minx,' he said with a smile as he tugged her gently out by the ankles before he scooped her up in his arms.

Ella giggled and patted his face again. '*Papà* finded me.'

Luca smiled, even though his chest ached at the irony of his little girl's words. 'Yes, Ella, *Papà* found you.'

He took her back to the bathroom and this time held on to her with one hand while he tried to open the change bag with the other. Ella wriggled and squirmed but somehow he managed to get a new nappy out as well as a change of clothes.

He decided upon inspection that it was a bath job, not a simple change of nappy. He ran a warm bath, carefully checking the temperature before he put Ella in. She laughed and kicked her legs under the water, splashing him in the process. He wished he had thought to buy some bath toys. He remembered having a rubber duck as a child and some little cups and a jug to play with. He made a mental note to get some the next day, as well as some baby bath instead of the heavily perfumed hotel bath foam in case it was too strong for her skin.

He thought of all the times Bronte must have done this, bathed and changed Ella, while juggling all the other things she had to do. No wonder she hadn't had time to sort out photos and albums.

'Out now?' Ella said, holding her arms up.

'Er... Right,' Luca said, reaching for a fluffy white towel. He wrapped it around her and lifted her out and carefully dried her. She fussed over getting dressed again, seeming to want to run around naked, but he somehow managed to convince her to wear a new nappy and another pair of leggings and matching dress.

'I'm hungry,' Ella announced matter-of-factly.

Luca wondered if room service catered for kids this young. What did kids of this age eat, anyway? He knew she had teeth; he had seen them shining like little pearls when she grinned so cheekily at him. He just hoped she didn't have any allergies he should know about. But surely Bronte would have told him. Mind you, Bronte hadn't told him much. She had stormed out and left him to it, no doubt to drive home her point about him knowing zilch about being a parent. It annoyed him that she was right. He didn't have a clue and was still running on instinct and doing a pretty poor job of it if the current position of Ella's nappy was any indication.

He adjusted it as well as he could and carried her back to the lounge. She sat on the floor and played with his phone while he used the hotel phone to dial room service. Within a very short time indeed a waiter came up to the suite with a suitable meal for a toddler, which Luca then proceeded to offer to Ella.

More food ended up on the floor than in her mouth, and he seriously considered giving her another bath as she had smeared yoghurt all over the front of her dress, not to mention her face and hands.

Luca wondered what to do next. Was she too young to be read to? Not that he had any children's books. He made another mental note about getting some tomorrow.

He sat her on his knee and made up a story to

keep her occupied. She looked up at him with a big smile and then settled her dark little head against his chest, right where his heart was beating. One of her thumbs crept up into her bee-stung mouth but he decided against pulling it out. He continued with his story until she finally fell asleep in his arms.

He held her for a long time, just sitting there feeling her slight weight on his lap, wishing he had been there for her birth, for every single moment of her life. How could he make it up to her? How could he make it up to Bronte? Would Bronte ever forgive him for cutting her from his life the way he had? He had thought he was doing the right thing at the time, but now he had to face the fact that a simple phone call would have changed everything. If anyone was to blame, it was him, not Bronte. She had done what she could do to reach him but he had made it impossible for her to get through. Even if she had written to him, he knew he would not have opened it. He had made a pact with himself and it had come back to bite him in the most devastating way.

Ella sighed and gave her tiny thumb another couple of substantial sucks before she settled back down to a deep and peaceful slumber.

Luca stroked his hand over her little silky head, his eyes misting as he thought of how much he had missed. He would do whatever it took to put things as right as they could be.

Whatever it took...

Bronte came back to the hotel feeling a little foolish for her outburst. She had worried the whole time she was away, thinking of Ella waking up disoriented and confused. What had she been thinking, rushing off in a tantrum like that? It surely wouldn't help Luca see her as a responsible and sensible young mother.

She got to the penthouse floor and, rather than use the swipe key, gave the door a soft knock so as not to wake Ella if she happened to still be asleep.

There was no answer.

She waited for another minute and then used the key. She walked into the lounge area to see Luca soundly asleep, with Ella, also out for the count, snuggled up against his chest. The pent-house looked as if a whirlwind had gone through it. There were toys and clothes strewn about the place and the remains of Ella's supper were still on one of the coffee tables.

Luca suddenly opened his eyes and, with his free hand, he quickly rubbed his face. 'How long have you been back?' he asked.

'Not long,' Bronte said, shifting her weight. 'Look, I'm sorry about storming out like that.'

He gave her a crooked smile. 'You did me a favour, Bronte. It's what I believe they call quality time, *sì*?'

She chewed at her bottom lip as she looked at what seemed to be smears of yoghurt all over the front of his designer business shirt. 'I hope it wasn't too steep a learning curve,' she said. 'Ella can have a mind of her own at times.'

'She's a Sabbatini,' he said with the same lop-sided smile. 'We're all a little bit stubborn about getting our own way.'

'Yes, well, I'm not going to argue with you about that,' Bronte said, folding her arms.

Luca looked down at the sleeping child. 'She's

a great little kid,' he said. 'I just wish I could have known about her from the start.'

'It was your choice to cut all contact.'

He raised his gaze back to hers. 'Yes, it was and I take full responsibility for it.'

Bronte frowned at him. 'So you're…you're apologising?'

He gave a small shrug. 'Would it help if I did?'

She drew in a tight little breath. 'Maybe, maybe not.'

Luca gently eased Ella off his lap and settled her onto the sofa, bunching up a couple of scatter cushions to keep her from rolling off the edge. Then he rose to his feet and came over to where Bronte was standing. 'About last night—' he began.

Bronte felt hot colour shoot to her cheeks. 'I'd rather not talk about it,' she said and took a step backwards but he caught her by the arm and held her in place.

'I think we do need to talk about it,' he said.

'It doesn't mean anything, you know,' she said, throwing him a cutting look. 'It was just sex.'

His eyes smouldered darkly as his thumb began to gently caress the underside of her wrist where her pulse was skyrocketing. 'It is never just sex with you, Bronte.'

She put her chin up. 'Maybe I've changed in the time we've been apart.'

He brought her wrist up to his mouth, pressing a soft kiss to the sensitive skin, his eyes holding hers mesmerised. 'Then if you have changed you will have no problem with our marriage being a real one,' he said. 'It will just be sex, nothing more, nothing less.'

Bronte felt the discomfort of being hoisted on one's own petard. 'I know what you're trying to do,' she said, pulling her hand away. 'You're trying to make me fall in love with you again.'

'I am trying to make you see how we can have a wonderful life together,' he said. 'I know there are hurts to deal with. I know you don't trust me not to walk out on you again. But, Bronte, I am not the same man I was two years ago.'

She rolled her eyes. 'People don't change that much, Luca. You'll have to do a whole lot more than talk if you want me to consider staying with you.'

A flinty look came into his eyes. 'Don't forget who you are dealing with, Bronte,' he said. 'I can still make things very difficult for you if you don't agree to marry me and move to Italy.'

Ella chose that moment to whimper. Bronte went to her and picked her up from the sofa, holding her close, as if daring Luca to take her from him. 'You can make me marry you, Luca,' she said bitterly. 'You can even make me live in a foreign country and make me play the role of the devoted wife. But you need to remember one thing: you can't—no matter what you do or say—make me love you again.'

Luca watched as she gathered Ella's things together, her stiff angry movements communicating her hatred of him. 'I would like to see Ella each day until we leave,' he said through tight lips.

'Fine,' she said, throwing him a filthy look over her shoulder as she stalked to the door.

'Bronte?'

She drew in a harsh breath and faced him with an irritated look on her face. 'Yes?'

His eyes bored into hers. 'Last night wasn't just sex. Not for me.'

Her expression faltered for a moment, her small perfect white teeth sinking into her full bottom lip. But just as quickly she reset her features into a tight little mask of indifference. 'I bet you say that to all your lovers,' she said and, without another word, left him with just the lingering fragrance of her perfume for company.

CHAPTER NINE

THE next three weeks passed in a blur of activity. Bronte's head was still spinning from the arguments she'd had with her mother over her acceptance of Luca's proposal. But in the end Bronte had refused to budge, knowing that if she said no to Luca she would not see Ella again.

He had made it perfectly clear: she was to marry him or suffer the consequences. It wasn't much of a choice, but then a secret part of her couldn't help but think of what life would be like married to him. That passionate interlude, which had left her body still smouldering in its wake all this time later, made her realise their marriage was not going to be the sterile paper agreement she had first thought. Even that evening at his hotel, even though he had only pressed his mouth to her wrist, she had felt every sensory nerve in her body stirring to throbbing, aching life.

However, since that night Luca had kept his distance physically. He kept their conversations brief and businesslike. He didn't touch Bronte once, not even to give her a kiss of greeting or goodbye. With Ella he was tender and attentive. He spent what time he could with her between appointments while Bronte watched in the background. It made her heart tighten every time she saw Ella's big blue eyes looking up at Luca so trustingly. His relationship with her was developing so rapidly, making Bronte feel as if Ella preferred her father now to her. Her little hands reached up to touch his stubbly face and her tinkling bell-like giggles brought a smile to his face, softening his features so much it made Bronte feel all the more wretched about how she had handled things.

Luca had organised an account at a high street wedding designer. Within moments of stepping into the smart boutique, Bronte found herself zipped into an exquisite gown that didn't just cost the earth but quite possibly half of the universe too. Other things were delivered to the studio or the granny flat: designer clothes, lacy lingerie, toys and clothes for Ella.

Two days before they were due to leave, Luca arranged to come to the flat for dinner. He wanted to be there in time to bathe and feed Ella, as he had done the night at the hotel, as he had been unable to do since due to business commitments.

He arrived just as Bronte's mother was leaving. Tina gave him a death stare as she began to pass by him on the doorstep but he stalled her by holding out an envelope to her.

'What is this?' Tina asked suspiciously.

'It is an all expenses paid trip to Italy for your daughter's wedding,' Luca said. 'I hope it will be the first of many visits to my homeland.'

Tina's mouth pursed, her gaze eyeing the envelope as if it was going to burst into flames as soon as she touched it.

'I want you to continue to be involved in Ella's life,' Luca said. 'You are her maternal grandmother. You have been a big influence in her life so far. I don't want that to change.'

Bronte watched from the sidelines as her mother's eyes moistened. Tina took the envelope with a grudging murmur of thanks and left.

Luca closed the door and turned to face Bronte. 'Do you think she will come?'

Bronte tucked a strand of loose hair back behind her ear. 'I've talked to her about it. She has a passport but she's never used it. She had planned to go on a trip to visit me in London but I came home before she could get there.'

A frown pulled at his brow, making his features darken. 'You can't resist reminding me of how I let you down, can you?' he asked.

'I wasn't doing any such thing,' she said. 'I simply told you—'

'*Papà!*' Ella toddled over, carrying the teddy bear Luca had given her, which was almost as tall as she was. '*Papà!*'

Luca smiled and scooped her up into his arms. '*Mio piccolo,*' he crooned. 'How is my baby girl?'

'She's been saying *Papà* a lot,' Bronte said. 'Especially when she sees the toys you bought her.'

He smiled and kissed Ella's button nose. 'I intend to give her everything money can buy,' he said.

Bronte unwound her twisted hands. 'Luca…I don't think it's wise to spoil her with too much too soon. She's very young. I don't want her to feel entitled to everything she sees. She needs to learn to appreciate things by learning to wait for them.'

He turned his black-brown gaze on her. It was hard, not soft and tender, and his smile had gone, leaving his mouth tight-lipped. 'Do not tell me what I can and cannot do with my very own child,' he said in a clipped tone.

Bronte raised her chin. 'She's a baby, Luca. She's not even two. She doesn't need a lot of expensive clothes and toys. She needs love and attention and security.'

'She will get that and more,' he said, putting the wriggling child back down on the floor to play with her toys.

'I am not sure how she is going to feel secure with us locked in a loveless, passionless marriage,' Bronte said, folding her arms across her middle.

Luca's eyes met hers, their smoky black depths sending a tingling feeling down her spine. 'You think our marriage will be without passion?' he asked.

Bronte felt her face crawl with colour. 'I'm not sure what to think. You've organised everything at breakneck speed. You've demanded I pack up my life here but I don't know what is expected of me on the other end.'

After a long moment he released a long sigh. 'I know this is hard for you, Bronte,' he said. 'It is hard for everyone. I feel for your mother, I really do. I feel for my mother and brothers and grandfather, who have missed out on all of Ella's babyhood so far. But you are Ella's mother and I am her father. There is no other way to do this.'

Bronte felt the sting of tears but fought them back. 'You want everything your way. You want control. I understand that, but it's hard for me. I've worked so hard for my career. But now I am expected to give it all up for what? A marriage that is doomed to fail.'

'It will not fail if we both work at it,' he said. 'I understand how important your career is to you. I am making arrangements for you to teach in Milan.'

'I don't speak the language,' Bronte said glumly. 'I'm not going to get very far without that.'

'You can take lessons,' he said. 'I want Ella to speak my language. It is important that she learns both English and Italian while she is young. It will help her if you speak both to her. I can organise a private tutor for you.'

'It seems to me you can organise just about anything,' she said, scowling.

'Not everything,' he said, raking a hand through his hair. 'There are some things money will never be able to buy.'

Bronte watched him crouch down to help Ella with a toy. He ruffled Ella's soft fluffy hair, his smile tender but touched with sadness at the same time. There were times when she thought he was locking her out. A mask would come down over his face, like a shutter on his emotions, leaving her wondering what it would take for him to trust her enough to tell her what he was really feeling.

Luca rose from the floor with Ella in his arms. 'I think she needs changing.'

'I'll do it.'

'I can manage,' he said. 'I got through it the last time. I need the practice, in any case.'

Bronte led him through to the small bathroom and handed him the baby bath solution she used to protect Ella's skin. 'I'll set out her night wear and a new nappy in the nursery for you,' she said.

When she came back Luca had Ella splashing in the bath. He was playing with a yellow duck, making quacking noises, to Ella's delight. It was a typical bath time scene, a loving father and a happy, contented infant having fun together. But Bronte felt shunted aside. She could imagine over time how Ella would no longer look to her for anything. It would all be about Luca. She understood how he wanted to make up for the time he had lost, but still she couldn't quell the feelings of insecurity that were plaguing her incessantly.

After Ella was dried and changed Bronte left Luca to read a story to Ella before tucking her into bed. She noticed it was an Italian one, the melodic-sounding words reminding her of how soon she would be locked out by language as well as Ella's burgeoning love for her father.

After checking on the casserole she had in the slow cooker, she waited for him in the living room, blindly leafing through a magazine for the want of something to do other than chew her nails.

Luca came out after a few minutes. 'She went to sleep like an angel,' he said.

'She's usually pretty good about going to sleep,' Bronte said. 'I guess I've been lucky that way. I'm not sure how I would have coped with a really difficult baby. It's been hard enough with her being so spirited and energetic.'

His mouth tightened. 'There you go again, playing the blame game. Painting yourself as the victim. We were both victims, Bronte. When are you going to see that?'

Bronte shot to her feet. 'When are you going to see that you can't just pick up where you left off? You broke my heart, Luca. You shattered my self-confidence. I don't want to get hurt again. I *won't* get hurt by you again.'

'Do you hate me that much?'

Bronte opened her mouth but then shut it, turning away so he couldn't see the glisten of tears in her eyes.

A taut silence beat for a moment or two.

'Bronte?'

'I think you already know the answer to that,' she said, still with her back to him.

The hairs on the back of her neck lifted long before his hands settled on her shoulders. How had her body known he was so close? A shiver went down her spine as she felt his strong tall body just behind her. If she leant backwards she would touch him, she would feel his heat and potency.

And she would be lost.

His warm breath skated over the sensitive skin of her neck as he spoke low and huskily near her ear. 'You don't really hate me, *cara*. You hate that you still want me.'

Bronte spoke through stiff lips. 'I don't want you. I loathe you.'

He gave a soft chuckle and slid his hands down the length of her arms, his fingers making a bracelet of steel around her wrists. 'Why don't you show me how much you loathe me?' he said, brushing up against her from behind.

She squeezed her eyes shut, trying to resist the temptation. She could feel his body responding to her closeness, his arrant maleness and the musky scent of his arousal. Her body crawled with desire, every nerve ending dancing with the need for more of his touch. Her breasts felt tight and achy, looking for the caress of his mouth and hands. Her inner core pulsed with need, a liquid hot need that had never really died down. It had smouldered like coals damped down in a fire, just waiting for the moment to spring back into leaping life.

'Go on,' he said, nibbling on her earlobe with the soft playful bite of his strong white teeth. 'Show me. I dare you.'

Bronte shivered again and her head fell to one side as his mouth moved over her neck before going to the top of her shoulder. She felt every movement of his lips, the soft brushes, the little nips, the slow drag and the sexy slide of his tongue. She was crumbling with need. She could feel her legs giving way…

He turned her in his arms and locked his eyes on hers. 'Double dare you,' he said softly, tauntingly, irresistibly.

Bronte felt her lashes go down as his head came down. She felt the breeze of his breath but he went no further. He hovered above her mouth, waiting for her to come to him. She held off for as long as she could but it was a battle she was never going to win. She wondered if that was why he had kept his hands off her for the last three weeks, to prove how little she could resist him when he turned on the charm.

Well, he was right. She couldn't resist him. She couldn't fight it any longer. With a soft sigh of surrender she reached up and pressed her lips against his.

It was a slow kiss at first, soft and sensual but

leisurely. Bronte wasn't sure when it changed or who had changed it. But suddenly there was nothing soft about it any more. There was hard urgency and heat and fiery purpose as his mouth commandeered hers. His tongue stroked for entry and slipped in when she gave it, teasing hers into an erotic mimic of what was to come.

Her body went wild with want. She snaked her arms around his neck, holding him closer, her pelvis rubbing up against the rock-hardness of his. Her breasts flattened against his chest, the tight nipples driving into him as he kissed her hotly and deeply.

She kissed him back with just as much urgency. She used her teeth to bite and nip, teasing him, leading him on until her body was screaming for release. She heard him groan deep in the back of his throat as her tongue darted and dived out of reach of his, only to come back to tease and taunt him with hot moist licks.

He swung her around, away from the wall and pressed her to the floor at their feet. Clothes were discarded piece by piece but there was no order to it. Bronte heard something rip but disregarded it. All she could think about was being pinned by his strong powerful body and being taken to paradise.

His hands were everywhere. One minute he was cupping her face, the next her breasts, his thumbs rolling over the pert nipples until she was gasping with soft little breaths of pleasure. His mouth took over from his hands, the hot moist caresses curling her toes and melting her spine.

She could feel the rough carpet on the tender skin of her back but she was beyond caring. She reached for him once he had shucked himself out of his trousers and underwear.

'If you are about to do what I think you are, I should warn you that you might get more than you bargained for,' he said in a voice that signalled how close he was to going over the edge.

Bronte sent him a sultry look from beneath her lashes. 'I'm sure you will recover quickly from the experience.'

'Don't do it, Bronte,' he bit out, his muscles clenching harder. 'Don't do it...*ahhh...*'

Bronte smiled to herself as he shuddered through his release. He might have kept his distance for the last three weeks but he was no less immune to her than she was to him.

He pushed her back down to the floor, leaning over her with his weight, his mouth starting to work its way down her body. 'My turn, I think,' he growled playfully.

Bronte felt a shiver rush down her body as his mouth closed over her breast. He sucked on her tantalisingly, drawing from her a whimpering cry. He went lower, down over her sternum, dipping his tongue into the tiny cave of her belly button before going deliciously, dangerously lower.

She drew in a sharp breath as his fingers gently opened her. She gripped his shoulders as his tongue brushed against her most sensitive point. A shudder went through her and then another as he repeated the caress again and again, picking up her internal rhythm, leading her step by inexorable step into the whirlpool of release. Her whole body shook with the explosion of pleasure that rippled through her. It was shameless, it was erotic, and it was primitive and unstoppable.

Bronte fell back but he wasn't finished with her. He moved back up her body, leaving her in no doubt of his rapid recovery. He was rock-hard and ready to go all over again. She gasped as he thrust into her deeply, the tight clutch of her inner muscles urging him on and on. She dug her fingers into his buttocks, holding him tight as he went harder. She felt every movement of his body in hers. Delight coursed through her, lifting her skin in delicate goosebumps of pleasure. It had always been this way between them: a roller coaster ride of passion and pleasure that knew no bounds.

'Tell me to slow down,' he said against her neck.

'Go faster,' she whispered back shamelessly.

He brought his mouth down hard on hers, kissing her as his body continued its passionate pounding within hers. She lifted her hips for each downward thrust, urging him on as her need for him climbed higher and higher.

The final lift-off was cataclysmic. It shook her from head to foot, every convulsion of her body sending shockwaves through his. Bursts of colour exploded in her head like a crazy kaleidoscope. Pleasure shot through her like a powerful drug, leaving her limbless and useless in his arms.

She felt him plunge into oblivion moments later, the quick, hard final thrusts pumping the life force from him until he collapsed against her.

As soon as it was over Bronte felt ashamed. Their coupling was about lust, not love. It was the same as in the past. She was a convenience, a plaything to entertain him. He didn't want anything else from her. He didn't love her. He was incapable of loving her. He was only marrying her to get his child.

'You are very quiet,' Luca said, raising himself up on his elbows to look down at her.

'Please get off me,' she said, pushing against him with her arms.

He controlled her flailing hands in one of his. 'Stop, damn it. What's the matter with you?'

She rolled her eyes. 'How can you ask that?'

'Bronte, we had consensual sex,' he said. 'You're surely not suggesting anything else?'

She glowered at him. 'This is all a game to you. You don't really want me as your wife. I'm just a means to an end. You get Ella with me thrown in for free. How convenient, a willing bed partner to entertain you whenever you feel like it.'

Luca studied her face for a moment. 'This is about the last three weeks, isn't it?'

She turned her head away so she couldn't look at him. He turned her head back, anchoring her chin so she wouldn't pull away. 'Look at me, Bronte,' he said. 'I've kept my distance to give you some space to think about the future. I had a lot on my mind, in any case. I had to cram six weeks of business into three. This is not all about you.'

'It's never been about me, has it?' she tossed back bitterly. 'Right from the start, our relationship has always been about you. What you want, what you were prepared to give or not give, to do or not do. It was never about what I wanted.'

This time when she pushed at him he let her go. She snatched up her clothes and disappeared into her room, shutting the door behind her.

Luca rolled onto his back and rubbed his hand down over his face. She was right, of course. He had never allowed her to dictate the terms of their previous relationship. He had always been the one to state the way things were going to be. He couldn't have handled her turning up unannounced at his London home. He couldn't have handled spending the night with her, or with anyone. He had never spent the night with anyone. It wasn't something he could have trusted himself to do until recently.

He got to his feet and pulled on his clothes. He used the bathroom and then checked on Ella. He stood, looking down at her sleeping angelic face, his heart feeling as if two large fingers had it in a hard pinch.

He heard a sound at the door and turned to see Bronte standing there. 'Is she all right?' she asked in a whisper.

'She's fine,' he said. 'I was just checking on her.'

She turned and went back to the kitchen. Luca heard her opening a cupboard and turning on a tap and then the hiss of the kettle as it came to a boil. He pressed a kiss to his fingertips and laid it gently on Ella's cheek before he left the room.

When he came into the kitchen Bronte's face was still looking stormy. She banged a cup down on the bench and then a tin of instant coffee, sending him a fiery look. 'Dinner's not quite ready but if you want a cup of coffee while you wait then this is all I've got. I don't have any wine.'

'Bronte, let's get something straight right from the start,' he said. 'I am not for a moment suggesting you haven't done a brilliant job of bringing up Ella to this point.'

She stood in a huffy silence, her slate-blue eyes wary as they held his.

'Ella is a contented and happy toddler,' he continued. 'She's a credit to you. I realise it must have been hard for you, alone and unsupported.

If I could change that, I would do so. We have to move forward with what we've got. And what we've got is a lot compared to most. What happened on that floor half an hour ago is proof of that.'

'What happened on that floor was exactly the sort of thing I expect from you,' she spat at him. She stirred her coffee until it splashed over the sides. The ping of her teaspoon when she set it down seemed to underline the silence.

'If you have something to say, then come right out and say it,' Luca said. 'Don't play word games with me.'

Her eyes flashed blue flames of hatred at him. 'I have carpet burn,' she said on a pout.

Luca felt his lips twitch. 'Show me.'

She backed away, her eyes widening. 'Get away from me.'

He cornered her against the work top, hip to hip, heat to heat. 'Turn around,' he commanded softly.

Her chest rose and fell against his, her eyes slowly filling with moisture. She blinked rapidly but a couple of tears escaped.

Luca blotted them with the pads of his thumbs, his heart feeling another tight pinch. 'Hey,' he said softly. 'Is this about carpet burn or something else?'

She shoved him away, catching him off guard. She stalked to the living room, her arms like a barricade over her middle. 'Don't you think it's about time you left?' she said, glancing pointedly at the clock. 'I would hate for you to turn into a werewolf or something once it gets to midnight. Ten-thirty was always the cut-off point, I seem to remember.'

Luca drew in a breath as he thought about the first time he had woken up to realise what he had done while asleep. His body had let him down in a way that shamed him even now. He refused to talk about it. He couldn't stand the pity or the revulsion. It was all behind him now and he wanted to keep it that way. 'I will leave when I am happy we are clear on a couple of things,' he said. 'Firstly, do you need some help with packing before we leave the day after tomorrow? I can't help you myself as I have some last minute business ends to tie up, but I can organise for someone to help you.'

'That won't be necessary,' she said stiffly.

'The second thing is the studio arrangements,' Luca said. 'I've spoken to Rachel. She's happy to continue with the lease. It will take time for her to find another business partner. I'm not charging her rent for the first six months so she can get on her feet.'

'Why would you do that?' she asked with a guarded look.

Luca shrugged. 'It seemed the least I could do, under the circumstances.'

'It doesn't seem like a very sound business decision,' she said, still with that same suspicious angling of her gaze.

'Not all the decisions I make are motivated by making money,' he said.

He went over to where he had tossed his jacket earlier and took out a velvet ring box. He brought it back to where Bronte was standing and handed it to her. 'You will need this,' he said. 'I hope it fits. I had to guess the size.'

'You could have asked me,' Bronte said,

not caring that she sounded churlish and ungrateful.

He set his mouth and turned away. 'You can smash it with a hammer if it's not to your taste.'

Bronte felt ashamed of herself as she opened the lid of the box. The most beautiful diamond lay blinking there like a bright star in its night sky of dark blue velvet. Her throat closed over as she took it out and slipped it on her finger. It was a perfect fit. Not too small, not too big—just right. She looked up to where he was standing staring out of the window to the front garden. 'Luca?'

He turned and strode over to scoop up his jacket and keys. 'I have to go,' he said. 'I will send a car for you and Ella on Friday at ten a.m. Don't be late.'

Bronte flinched as the front door snapped shut behind him. Her heart sank as she heard his car roar off down the street, and her tears fell freely as the low growling sound slowly faded into the distance.

CHAPTER TEN

WHEN Luca arrived in a chauffeur driven car on Friday morning there were too many people about for her to deliver the apology she had spent the last two days rehearsing. By the time she had said a tearful goodbye to her mother and Rachel, Ella needed her attention. When they got to the airport Luca was busy with officialdom so it wasn't until they were on the private jet, secluded in their own quarters, that she finally found herself alone with him, apart from Ella sleeping in a cot nearby.

'Luca…' she began with a quick dart of her tongue over her lips. 'I wanted to apologise to you about the way I spoke to you when you gave me the engagement ring.'

He turned one more page of the document he was reading and she heard him release a slow breath before he lifted his head to look at her sitting opposite him. 'Forget about it,' he said and returned to his work.

She twirled the ring on her finger, her teeth gnawing at her lip as she watched him leaf through the lengthy document. The silence hummed… Well, perhaps it was really the jet that was humming as it levelled out after take-off but, all the same, Bronte felt as if a chasm had opened up between them.

'I just wanted to say I'm sorry,' she said after a long moment. 'It's a beautiful ring. It must have cost a fortune.'

He turned another page without looking up. 'It did.'

Bronte moistened her lips again and watched him for a little while. He was frowning with concentration, his mouth flat and serious and his clean-shaven jaw tight. There were lines of tiredness about his eyes, which made her wonder if he had slept at all over the last couple of nights.

'What are you reading?' she offered after another long silence.

'Nothing important.'

'Is it to do with the hotel developments in Australia?'

He closed the folder and met her eyes across the wide space between them. 'Yes,' he said. 'Now, why don't you lie back and have a sleep while Ella's down?'

Bronte twirled her ring again. 'You're angry with me.'

'Is that a statement or a question?'

'It's an observation,' she said.

He gave her a wry smile that didn't reach his eyes. 'And why would I be angry with you, do you think?'

She let out a choppy sigh. 'Because I've been an absolute cow about all this.' She waved her hand to encompass their luxurious surroundings. 'You've gone to a lot of trouble to arrange everything and I haven't thanked you once.'

'You don't have to thank me,' he said.

'But you've spent heaps on me and Ella too,' she said. 'And buying Mum that ticket. She's going to come to the wedding. I didn't think she would but she told me just as I was leaving. I don't know how to thank you for doing all that for me…for us…'

Luca put the folder on the seat next to him and, unclipping his seatbelt, stood up and came over to sit beside her. He took her hand in his and began idly stroking it with his thumb. 'The money is nothing to me, Bronte. It's not what counts in life.'

Bronte looked into his dark eyes and felt something shift in her chest. 'You really love Ella, don't you?' she asked softly.

'Now that is definitely an observation,' he said with another wry smile. 'There's no question about it. I love her more than life itself.'

Bronte felt an ache deep inside. If only he would say the same about her. How she had longed to hear those words. She looked down at their joined hands; hers looked so small inside the shelter and protection of his. His skin was so dark, so masculine with its sprinkling of black hair, while hers was so soft and smooth and creamy-white.

She felt a little quiver of awareness when she met his eyes again. Their dark depths reflected everything that had occurred between them two days ago. She could feel the rush of her blood and imagined his body doing the same. Was he remembering how it felt to be joined in out of control passion? Was he remembering the electric shock of intimate contact, the roller coaster ride of release that was as mind blowing as any illicit drug could be?

Luca took her chin between his finger and thumb, a soft tether that had an undercurrent of desire she could feel through his skin to hers. 'I have my own apology to deliver,' he said in a gravel-rough tone.

Bronte felt her face heating. 'You don't have to apologise for anything.'

'Oh, but I do,' he said in the same deep husky voice as he brushed his thumb over her bottom lip. 'I was rough with you. I could have hurt you.'

Bronte longed to slip her tongue out to touch his thumb. 'You didn't,' she said in a breathless whisper.

His thumb stilled and his eyes centred on hers.

'You mentioned something about carpet burn the other night.'

She lowered her gaze, hot colour surging into her cheeks. 'I just said that to annoy you.'

He tipped her chin up again, holding her gaze with the dark intensity of his. 'I really meant it when I said you should get some sleep,' he said. 'There's a bed through there in the curtained section next to Ella.'

'But I don't feel tired,' she said as her gaze slipped to his mouth.

His mouth turned up at the corners in a sexy smile. 'Then maybe I can think of something to occupy you until you do.'

Bronte's heart gave a little sideways movement as her eyes came back to his. 'You mean…here? In the plane?'

His eyes were glinting. 'No one will disturb us. We have this entire section to ourselves.'

She gave him a shy look. 'You really think of everything, don't you?'

He pressed a kiss to the tips of her fingers. 'Go and get ready,' he said. 'I will be with you in a minute.'

* * *

Bronte yawned and stretched a few hours later. Her body was still tingling from Luca's passionate but exquisitely tender lovemaking. She turned her head to look at him. He was lying on his back, his eyes closed and his chest rising and falling as he slept.

She smiled and softly traced a fingertip down his sternum, all the way down to his belly button. This was the longest time she had ever spent in bed with him. Seven hours, almost a complete night.

She trailed her fingers over his flat dark nipples and, as she went a little lower, she felt him flinch but his eyes remained closed. She circled his navel a couple of times, lightly, teasingly. Then she went even lower, millimetre by millimetre, watching as his abdominal muscles tightened as her caresses approached his growing erection. She took him in her hand, squeezing ever so gently, her fingers sliding down the shaft, her belly turning to liquid as he swelled even further.

He suddenly moved, rolling her on to her back in a quick movement, his body surging into hers in one slick hard thrust that sent the air right out of her lungs. She gasped in delight as he set a steady pace, her already damp body making it easy for him to gain momentum. She scored her nails down his back as the sensations rippled through her. She was climbing to the summit so quickly, all her senses spinning in the wake of his touch. His mouth captured hers, subjecting it to a sensual assault that made the hair on her head lift in pleasure.

Her body split into a thousand pieces as she came. Her mind blacked out in that moment of sheer ecstasy, every muscle, nerve and sinew twitching in the aftermath. Luca followed with his own release, a deep pumping of his body within hers, his agonised groan of pleasure sending a shiver of reaction straight down Bronte's spine.

Long minutes passed.

Bronte was content to lie in the circle of his arms, playing mind games with herself about him loving her and wanting her back in his life for good, even if Ella wasn't an issue. Her love for him had never really gone away. She had blocked it out in order to protect herself. She still had nightmares about him leaving her again. Any rejection was hard to take, but one that she had been more or less waiting for right from the start for some reason had been so much worse. It had destroyed her trust and her self-confidence had never really recovered. Telling him how she felt was out of the question. She had told him too much too soon in the past and look where that had taken her. No, this time she would play it cool. No hearts worn on the sleeve, no confessions of eternal love. No long-term promises. She would be cool and clinical about their arrangement. A marriage that would give her the security she had longed for, financial if not emotional. She had watched her mother struggle all of her life to put food on the table. At least Bronte would not have those sorts of worries to deal with. It was a compensation of sorts, but not exactly as reassuring as she would have liked.

Luca lifted his head and pressed a kiss to the end of Bronte's nose. 'Hey,' he said.

'Hey yourself,' she said back.

His eyes held hers for several beats before he spoke. 'Are you currently on the Pill?'

Bronte felt a little flutter of unease. 'Yes, but only a low dose one to control period pain.'

'If you were to fall pregnant you wouldn't get period pain, though, would you?' he said.

A small frown began to pull at her brow. 'What exactly are you saying, Luca?' she asked.

He brushed some tousled strands of her hair back from her face. It was a stalling tactic, Bronte suspected, which made her angry. Why couldn't he just touch her because he couldn't help it?

'I am saying we should maybe think about trying for another child,' he said, this time lazily curling a strand of her hair around one of his fingers. 'I missed out on the first year and two months of Ella's life. If we were to have a brother or sister for Ella it would make me feel less of that loss, I am sure. The gap between them would be ideal. If you were to fall pregnant more or less straight away, she would be out of nappies and a little more independent when the baby arrives.'

Bronte put her hands on his chest to try and push him off her. 'Let me up.'

He refused to budge, pinning her with his body, his eyes locked on hers. 'What's the problem, *cara*?' he asked.

She gave him a fulminating look. 'You've got it all planned, haven't you?'

He let her hair fall from his fingers. 'I haven't planned anything, Bronte. I am merely suggesting—'

Without the tether of her hair, this time she managed to wriggle out from under him. She scrambled to her feet and grabbed a bathrobe with his family's insignia on it, tying it about her waist with angry, jerky movements. 'I am not some stupid breeding machine,' she said through tight lips.

He reached for the matching bathrobe and slipped it on with much less haste than Bronte had. 'You have an amazing ability to twist my words,' he said with a thread of anger stitched in his voice. 'You will be my wife in a matter of days. It is not unreasonable for me to suggest we think about having another baby some time in the future. It doesn't have to be straight away. I just think it is something we should seriously think about, especially since I missed out on all this before.'

Bronte's eyes flashed. 'It's totally unreasonable! I'm not ready to have another baby.'

He placed his hands on his hips, his legs splayed in a let's-talk-about-this pose. 'What are your main objections?' he asked.

She stared at him for a tense moment before she blew out a breath. 'How can you ask that?'

'Bronte, I want more children,' he said with an intractable set to his mouth. 'I would like to have a son.'

Bronte sent him a death glare. 'So your daughter isn't good enough? Is that it?'

His eyes rolled upwards in an impatient manner. 'There you go again, twisting my words. I love Ella. She's my whole world. I'm just saying I would like to have a son if fate or destiny or God or whatever allows it.'

'We might have several daughters,' she said with a hitch of her chin.

'Then I will love each one with all my heart.'

But what about me? Bronte silently asked. *Will you ever love me with all your heart?* 'I can see why your sister-in-law left your brother,' she said with a cynical twist to her mouth. 'Is it a Sabbatini condition upon marriage to produce an heir and a spare as soon as possible?'

He pushed his thick black hair back off his face. 'Maybe we should discuss this some other time,' he said.

'No,' Bronte said. 'Let's discuss it now. I am not going to be an incubator. I am not going to agree to bring another child into this relationship unless I am convinced it is stable and secure.'

'Our marriage will be more secure than most,' he pointed out. 'You will want for nothing. Most women would give anything to be in your position.'

Bronte folded her arms. 'Money means nothing to me, Luca. You should know that by now. It doesn't impress me.'

'I know that,' he said. 'I admire that about you. I've always admired that about you. It's the one thing that has always set you apart from all the other women I have been involved with before you came along.'

She felt the wind drop right out of her self-righteous sails. 'You say that as if there has been no one since me,' she said, looking down at the floor.

There was a short but telling silence.

Bronte slowly brought her gaze back to his. He was looking at her with an unreadable expression on his face. 'Luca?'

His slowly spreading smile was self-deprecating. 'Not quite the bed-hopping girl-in-every-port playboy profile you were expecting, is it, Bronte?'

She looked at him in confusion. 'But you were in America… Your housekeeper told me about your…your mistress…'

'There wasn't a mistress.'

Bronte wanted to believe him. Everything in her wanted to believe him but her mind just couldn't get around it, couldn't accept it. 'Then why…?' She left the question hanging in the air between them.

He rubbed a hand over his in-need-of-a-shave face, an abrasive sound that seemed louder than it should have in the silence. 'I was in America for something else. Something personal.'

Bronte continued to look at him with wide uncertain eyes. 'You didn't think you could tell me at the time?' she asked.

He gave his head a little shake. 'I told no one, not even my family.'

She drew in an uneven breath. 'I don't understand, Luca. Why did you push me away? You were so callous about it. You hurt me more than anyone, more than I thought it was possible to be hurt by another person.'

His expression became shadowed with regret. 'I realise that. I wish I could change what happened but I can't. I did what I thought was best under the circumstances.'

Bronte turned away, her arms still wrapped around her middle as if to hold her hurt and anger close. She wasn't quite ready to let it go. 'Are you going to tell me what you were doing in the US?'

It was a full thirty seconds before he answered. 'I had an operation.'

She turned back to face him. 'What sort of operation?'

Again he hesitated before he spoke. 'I had an ablation done for nocturnal epilepsy.'

Bronte's forehead wrinkled. 'You had… *epilepsy*?'

'Not the usual type, but yes,' he said, looking grim.

She continued to look at him in stupefaction. 'You had it the whole time we were together and said *nothing*?'

'What could I say?' he asked bitterly. 'Watch out in case I have a fit while I'm asleep, lose control, and knock out some of your teeth or break your nose with one of my flailing, jerk-ing limbs? For God's sake, Bronte, I was trying to protect you. Do you know how many times I woke up to find the bedside lamp shattered or the alarm clock on the floor in pieces? I was living a nightmare each night of my life since I was twenty-seven, when I suffered what I thought was a minor head injury. I came off my mountain bike. I didn't even go to the hospital. It was a week or so later that I had my first fit. It happened in the middle of the night. I woke up…' He stopped and clawed a hand through his hair as if the memory of it was torturing him. 'I woke up and my life as I had known it had suddenly changed. I won't embarrass you with the sordid details. From that moment on, I couldn't spend the night with anyone. I daren't fall asleep until I was alone. I couldn't trust my body.'

Bronte let out a shocked breath. 'I don't understand why you didn't tell me. You could have saved us both all of this hurt and heartbreak if you had shared this with me.'

His brows narrowed the distance between his eyes. 'I did it for you, Bronte, can't you see that? I couldn't live with myself if I hurt you physically. You don't know what it was like. I lost who I was. I sometimes became irritable and bad-tempered before a fit came on. Sometimes I didn't get any notice at all. It would just happen. I felt like half a man. I was terrified the press would find out. Can you imagine what they would have done with that?'

'Luca—' Bronte moistened her lips '—I understand how awful it must have been, but you made it a thousand times worse by not telling me. If you had just explained why you were the way you were I would have loved you anyway.'

His eyes took on a hollow look. 'You don't understand what I was facing, Bronte. You can never understand. I knew the operation was an option I could take. The chance came for me to go to the States to have it done. I only had a week or so to prepare. There were risks involved, as there are with any surgery. You have to remember I watched my father become an invalid after his accident. He was completely helpless. He had to wear nappies, for God's sake. I had to spare you that. I couldn't have you tied to me in case something went wrong.'

'But it didn't,' Bronte said, still unable to let go of her hurt at being shut out at such a crucial time in his life. 'You ruined both of our lives by being so one-sided. You were only thinking about yourself, not me.'

'Damn it, I was thinking about you,' he said. 'I thought about you all the time. How I missed you. How I wanted you back, but I couldn't do it until I knew for sure I was cured.'

'You know, Luca, it's not really about what you had done in the States,' she said tightly. 'The issue is, you didn't trust me enough with what was going on in your life. I was your part-time plaything. The only intimacy we shared was physical. You weren't available emotionally then and you're not available now.'

His mouth flattened as his hand raked through his hair again. 'I couldn't offer you a future I didn't even know for sure I had.'

Bronte sent her eyes heavenwards. 'Oh, please. Give me a break, Luca. You know nothing of how relationships work, of how real love works. You wanted everything on your terms and you got it. It's your fault you missed out on Ella's first year of life, not mine.'

The sound of Ella waking in the curtained section next door brought an end to the conversation. Luca muttered something about it being his turn to see to her and strode out, brushing past Bronte's shoulder as he went.

She let out a sigh as she sat back down on the crumpled bed. She looked at the depression where Luca's head had been lying on the pillow. She picked up the pillow and hugged it to her chest, breathing in his inimitable scent that lingered on the fine Egyptian cotton

CHAPTER ELEVEN

BRONTE barely had time to shower and dress before it was announced they were beginning their descent in to the airport at Milan. Once Ella was safely strapped in her seat and sucking on a bottle of juice to protect her ears from the pressure in the cabin, Bronte had little time to speak to Luca. He was sitting in a brooding silence, his documents open again on his lap, his eyes scanning them with deep concentration.

He too had showered and changed and was now dressed in chinos and a blue open neck shirt, the light colour highlighting his tanned skin. He looked tense, however, and Bronte didn't know if it was because he was introducing his wife-to-be and his daughter to his family or because of the words they had exchanged earlier. She had thought about the operation he had said he'd had. His thick hair covered the scars but the mental scars were something she wasn't sure would ever go away. The more she thought about what he had gone through, the more she regretted how she had handled his revelation. He was a proud and very private man. No wonder he hadn't been featured in the press for the last two years. He would have done anything to keep such a personal thing away from the gossip pages.

The wall was back up between them and Bronte felt bad she might have been the one to put it there this time. She had allowed her anger and hurt to ruin everything. Maybe her touchiness was one of the reasons he hadn't told her in the first place. She had pushed and pushed him two years ago, wanting more and more from him, and he had kept closing off. It all made perfect sense now. Why he would suddenly cancel dates at the last moment, or why he would turn up on edge and tetchy, his tongue sharper than normal. A couple of days later he would be back and she had been so desperate she had capitulated as if nothing had changed. If only she had delved a little deeper. If only she had thought of reasons other than another woman, maybe none of this heartache would have happened.

She shifted in her seat and delicately cleared her throat. 'Luca?'

He kept his place on the document with his hand and looked across at her. 'Don't worry about meeting my family,' he said. 'They will accept you without question.'

She bit down on her lip. 'Actually, I wasn't worried about that… Well, maybe a little…' She took a little breath and continued, 'Are you all right… I mean…now?'

He frowned for a long moment without answering.

Bronte ran her tongue over her lips. 'The operation? The ablation? Was it a success?'

Nothing moved on his face, not a muscle, apart from those he needed to speak. 'Yes.' He paused for a nanosecond. 'Yes, it was.'

Bronte looked down at her hands. 'I wish you had told me…' she said softly. 'At the time, I mean…but I understand why you didn't.'

It seemed a long time before he answered. 'I wish I had too, *cara*.'

Luca's older brother was at the airport gate to meet them. Bronte could see the family likeness straight away. They were both tall and dark-haired with strong uncompromising jaws and a prominent nose and deep brown intelligent eyes.

After brief introductions were made, Giorgio took her hand and leaned forward to kiss her on both cheeks. 'Welcome to the family,' he said in a beautifully cultured voice, not unlike Luca's.

'Thank you,' Bronte said and watched as Giorgio's gaze went to Ella, who was kicking her legs in the pushchair and chortling.

He bent down and smiled a white-toothed smile that made his eyes crinkle up at the corners. There was a shadow of sadness there, Bronte thought, as he took one of Ella's tiny hands in his. 'This must be my little niece Ella,' he said.

Ella smiled widely and held her arms up high. 'Up, up.'

'May I?' Giorgio addressed Bronte.

'Of course,' she said, quickly unclipping Ella's pushchair straps. 'She hates being confined in there now that she's walking.'

'Ah, a little independent miss, eh, Ella?' Giorgio said as he gathered the child in his arms.

Luca smiled cautiously as he laid a hand on his older brother's shoulder. 'How are you?'

Giorgio gave a could-mean-anything shrug. 'I am fine. Why would I not be? She left me, not me her. It's apparently what she wants. I can stall and I am doing so, but only for so long. I am fed up with it, frankly.'

Luca's smile fell away, along with his hand. 'I'm sorry.'

'Don't be.' Giorgio's tone was curt. 'It's for the best.'

Bronte exchanged a short look with Luca. She saw the concern in his expression and grimaced in empathy. He came over and slipped an arm around her waist. She didn't move away but instead found herself nestling against his warm strength as they made their way out to where his brother had parked the car.

The drive to Luca's villa was interspersed with Giorgio pointing out various landmarks and points of interest. 'Have you been to Milano before, Bronte?' he asked.

'Just the once,' she said, chancing a quick glance at Luca, sitting silently beside his brother in the passenger seat. 'It was just a quick stop-over really. I didn't do any sightseeing. There wasn't time.'

'You will have to get Luca to show you around,' Giorgio said, quickly and expertly checking the traffic before he merged into the next lane. 'Our mother will look after Ella for you. She is bursting with excitement about finding out she finally has a granddaughter. She has bought so many toys her villa looks like Hamleys in London.'

Within a few minutes Giorgio pulled into Luca's villa grounds. On the outside it was much the same as it had been two years ago, but Bronte hadn't seen inside on her one and only visit in the past. Built on four levels, it had multiple bedrooms and formal and informal rooms for entertaining. It was breathtakingly decorated inside; no expense had been spared to turn it into a villa of distinction. Priceless works of art hung from the walls, marble statues and brass and bronze figures and busts were show-cased here and there. The marbled foyer and winding staircase would have been intimidating, except Luca's housekeeper—Bronte assumed it was his housekeeper—had placed various vases of late summer roses all throughout, their delicate fragrance giving the villa a welcoming atmosphere.

Bronte turned a full circle in wonder. 'It's beautiful...'

Giorgio tickled Ella under the chin before he turned to look at Bronte with a quizzical look on his face. 'Hasn't Luca brought you here before?' he asked. 'When you said you'd been to Milano, I assumed you meant for a night or two here with him.'

Bronte didn't look in Luca's direction but she could feel the weight of his gaze. 'No,' she said, keeping all trace of emotion out of her voice. 'He didn't get around to it.'

Giorgio handed a wriggling Ella back to Bronte. 'I had better leave you two to settle in before our mother and grandfather arrive,' he said.

'Aren't you joining us for dinner?' Luca asked.

Giorgio shook his head. 'No, I have a prior engagement.'

Luca's brows snapped together. 'You're seeing someone?'

Giorgio's expression hardened. 'Maya is divorcing me, Luca. It wasn't my idea. It's time to move on. It's over.'

'But surely it's too early to be seen out with someone—'

Giorgio exchanged a few rapid fire sentences in Italian. Luca's response was clipped and the air almost crackled with tension for a few tense seconds.

Bronte was glad when Ella started to grizzle. After a tersely delivered goodbye sent in Bronte's direction Giorgio left with a closing of the front door that could almost be described as a slam.

Luca's expression was thunderous as he came over to pick up their cases.

'Is everything all right?' she asked tentatively.

He threw her a disgusted look. 'My brother is a stubborn fool.'

'I am sure it's not wise to get involved in someone else's relationship,' she said. 'They have to work it out themselves.'

He looked at her for a long moment. 'Maybe you're right,' he said on a heavy sigh.

Bronte looked around. 'Don't you have any household staff any more?'

'I wasn't expected back until the week after next,' he said. 'My mother has loaned me her housekeeper until mine gets back from leave.'

She frowned as she tucked Ella closer on her left hip. 'Is it the same one who turned me away at the door when I came to tell you about Ella?'

He gave her an unreadable look. 'No,' he said and turned and led the way upstairs.

Ella was in the wrong time zone for sleep so Bronte decided to keep her up until Luca's mother and grandfather arrived. Apart from showing her around the villa earlier, she hadn't seen much of Luca. She assumed he was answering emails or returning phone calls from his large study on the second floor.

He had shown her to the master bedroom suite and Bronte was in there, thinking about unpacking with Ella sitting on the floor at her feet, when there was a soft knock at the door. A woman in her late fifties or early sixties introduced herself as Rosa, the Sabbatini housekeeper. She gushed over Ella, telling Bronte in reasonably good English about her own soon-to-arrive grandchild. Bronte liked Rosa right from the start. There was nothing haughty or judgemental about her.

'You are a very lucky woman,' Rosa said as she expertly unpacked the first of the suitcases while Bronte chose something to wear for the evening's dinner. 'Luca is a good man, *sì*?'

Bronte stretched her lips into a smile as she handed Ella another toy. 'Yes, yes, he is.'

'He loves his little *bambino*,' Rosa continued, looking down at Ella with a smile. 'He has always loved children. Giorgio is the same.' She tut-tutted as she placed a shirt on the to-be-ironed pile. 'Me, I don't believe in divorce, not unless one party has been unfaithful or violent or has an addiction problem. Marriage has to be worked at.'

'Maybe they fell out of love,' Bronte offered.

Rosa gave her a frowning look from beneath her brows. 'Love is like a garden. It needs nurturing even when it changes with the seasons. Luca won't let you go so easily. He is stubborn at times but not as bull-headed as his older brother. And then there's Nic.' She smiled indulgently as she folded another top. 'He's a wild one, that one. It will take a very special woman to tame him.'

Bronte thought about how different Luca's life was from hers. He had a loving family, money to burn and staff waiting on his every need. She, on the other hand, had grown up feeling the pressure of being an only child to a single mother who hadn't yet learned to untie the apron strings.

'Would you like me to press that for you?'

Rosa asked, pointing at the black dress Bronte had clutched to her chest.

'Oh… No, I can do it.'

Rosa plucked it out of Bronte's grasp. 'I am here to help you, Signorina Bennett. I will take Ella with me so you can shower and dress in peace. Luca told me the nanny won't be starting work until Monday.'

Bronte blinked. 'The nanny?'

Rosa scooped up Ella off the floor and planted her firmly on one generous hip. 'He did not tell you?'

'No, he did not.'

'Ah, here he is now,' Rosa said and, smiling at Luca, left the room with Ella giggling as she tried to pull at Rosa's earring.

Bronte faced him squarely. 'What is this about a nanny?'

He closed the door of the bedroom, his expression shuttered as usual. 'You have some objection to having help with Ella?' he asked.

'Of course I do,' she said, glaring at him. 'My main one being I haven't been consulted. You keep doing everything over my head.'

'Francesca comes with very good recommendations,' he said. 'She has a lot of experience. I am sure you will get along just fine.'

'That's not the point,' Bronte said. 'Why didn't you discuss it with me?'

'What is there to discuss?' he said. 'You had your mother on call in Australia. I thought you would need similar backup here. You are intending to teach, remember? How do you expect to do that with Ella in tow?'

Bronte crossed her arms and paced the room. 'I hate leaving Ella with anyone,' she said. 'I love teaching, don't get me wrong, it's just that I never imagined I would have to sacrifice so much of my time—the time I would rather spend with Ella.' She turned and looked at him. 'I know you feel cheated out of the first year and a bit of Ella's life but I've been cheated too. I wasn't there the day she took her first step. My mother was. I will always feel guilty about that.'

Luca came over and unpeeled her arms, sliding his hands down them so he could encircle her wrists with his fingers. 'We have both missed out due to circumstances out of our control,' he said. 'But we have the future to put what we can right.'

She looked up at him with uncertainty in her slate-blue eyes. 'It would be different if we were in love.'

Luca felt his heart flinch as if someone had struck it. He schooled his features into impassivity and dropped his hands from hers. 'I am sure we will muddle along quite nicely,' he said. 'Thankfully, love isn't a requirement for good sex.'

'Sex is hardly a good basis for marriage,' she said with heightened colour. 'What happens when the lust dies down? Will you find someone else to keep your needs met?'

'That will depend entirely on you,' he said. 'I am not a great believer in extramarital affairs. Someone always wants more than can be given. People get hurt, and not just the adults. But if you no longer want to continue a physical relationship with me then I will have to consider my options.'

She gave her head a little toss but he saw the

flash of fire in her gaze as she turned away.
Jealousy was always a good sign. It might not
mean she loved him the way she used to do,
but it meant she wasn't prepared to share him,
which was a very good start.

'I'll let you know,' she said in a stiff little
voice.

Luca smiled to himself. 'So you're happy to
share my bed for the time being?' he asked in
an even tone.

She turned back to look at him, the twin spots
of colour on her cheeks still glowing red-hot. 'It
amuses you that I am so weak, doesn't it?'

'I'm not amused,' he said, trying for deadpan.
'I'm delighted.'

She gave him a withering look. 'It's just lust,
nothing else. I think you should know that. It's
probably hormones or something.'

'Of course.'

She searched his features for a moment, her
eyes narrowing slightly. 'What are you smiling
about?'

'Was I smiling?' he asked with a guileless look.

'Not on the outside, but you are on the inside,' she said. 'I can see the glint in your eyes.'

Luca placed his hands on her shoulders. 'That's because I am imagining you without those clothes on with me in the shower.' He brought her up close to his body, one of his hands slipping beneath her silky dark hair, the other pressing against the small of her back. 'We have just enough time if we hurry.'

Her eyes flickered and then dropped to his mouth. 'It's hormones. Definitely hormones. I'm sure of it,' she said in a soft, breathless little voice.

'Hormones sound good to me,' Luca said and, swooping down, covered her mouth with his.

Bronte took a deep breath as Luca led her down the stairs to meet his mother and grandfather, who had just arrived. She could hear them chatting with Rosa in the *salone*, their voices full of excitement and anticipation.

Luca had Ella in his arms and his mother rushed up to him as soon as the door opened. 'Luca, *caro*,' she choked as she reached for Ella.

'She is the image of Chiara. Oh, dear God, how I have longed for this moment.'

Bronte stood to one side as Luca's grandfather cooed over Ella. She could see where Luca got his good looks from. Salvatore Sabbatini night be nudging ninety but he was still a tall man of proud bearing. He had the same air of authority about him that both Luca and Giorgio had. His hair was grey and his face a little lined but, even at that great age, he was still worth a double take.

Luca's mother too had clearly been a beauty in her day. She was small and delicately made, with salt and pepper hair that should have aged her but somehow didn't. She had beautiful skin and had a natural elegance about her.

'*Mamma, Nonno,*' Luca said, cupping Bronte's elbow. 'This is my fiancée, Bronte Bennett.'

Salvatore was the first to come over. He took Bronte's hand and, just as Giorgio had done earlier that day, leaned forward to kiss her on both cheeks. 'This is a very happy day for us,' he said in heavily accented but still perfect English. 'You have blessed us with Giovanna's first grandchild and my first great-grandchild. I have lived for this day. I cannot tell you how it makes me feel to know the bloodline will continue.'

Bronte knew her smile looked a little forced but she just couldn't help it. 'I am sorry you haven't met her until now.'

'Better than not at all,' Salvatore said.

There was a small silence.

'*Mamma,*' Luca prompted.

Giovanna Sabbatini was still holding Ella, looking very much as if she was not going to let her go. 'I am glad you finally decided to tell our son he was a father,' she said. 'But did you not think of how you were not just robbing him of all those months of her life but his family as well?'

'*Mamma—*' Luca's voice was deep and full of admonition '—this is not the time to—'

'It's all right, Luca,' Bronte said sending him a pained look. 'Your mother is absolutely right. I didn't think about anyone else at the time. If I had, it might have turned out very differently.'

Giovanna refused to be mollified. 'My oldest

son is going through a very painful and, in my opinion, totally unnecessary divorce,' she said. 'That might not have happened if Luca had known about his daughter before now.'

Bronte felt her back come up. 'I hardly think it is my fault your son and his wife spilt up,' she said. 'I accept that I was wrong not to work harder at contacting Luca, but I was angry and hurt about him breaking off our relationship.'

Salvatore placed a firm but gentle fatherly hand on Bronte's shoulder. 'Forgive my daughter-in-law,' he said. 'This is an emotional time for us all. We have been through a lot with almost losing Luca two years ago and, of course, my son, his father, Giancarlo five years ago now. And before that we lost little Chiara, my grand-daughter. I am not sure if you know about her. It was a long time ago but we live with it daily. Ella is a blessing God has sent to us to help heal our pain.'

Almost losing Luca... The rest of Salvatore's words faded as those three reverberated inside Bronte's head. They had almost *lost* him? She looked at Luca, standing so silently, a brooding frown stitched on his brow. She swallowed and tried to focus on what Salvatore was saying but her mind kept drifting back to those three ominous-sounding words.

Dinner was a bit of a strained affair. Bronte had no appetite and, although Luca's grandfather was charming and did everything in his power to include her in the conversation, it was clear Giovanna was not going to budge. Bronte could understand it, being a mother herself. She decided to be as patient as possible and not be drawn into any comebacks she might have cause to regret later. After all, this was to be her mother-in-law, not the easiest of relationships at the best of times.

Once Luca's mother and grandfather had left and Ella was sleeping soundly in her cot, Bronte waited for Luca in the bedroom. He came in after a good hour, which made her wonder if he had been hoping she would fall asleep before he got there.

'Luca,' she said without preamble, 'I want to know what your grandfather meant about almost losing you two years ago.'

The shutters came down over his face and his mouth went into a flat line. 'My grandfather spoke out of turn,' he said. 'So did my mother. I am sorry about how she behaved. She will soften eventually. She was the same with my brother's wife Maya. Although I can't say they are all that close now.'

'Look, I recognise the mother lion thing,' she said. 'But that's not what we are discussing. What happened, Luca?'

'Nothing happened,' he said, averting his gaze. 'My grandfather exaggerated the situation.'

'You're lying.'

'You are imagining things,' he said and pulled back the covers.

'I am not getting into bed with you until you tell me what happened to you, Luca,' she said with a determined jut of her chin.

His hand dropped from the covers, his eyes locking with hers. 'You want to fight or make love?' he asked.

Bronte felt a shiver of reaction course down her spine at his challenging look. 'I don't want to fight you, Luca, I want to understand you. You keep shutting me out. You've always done it. You always keep something back of yourself.'

He drew in a breath at the same time as his hand scored a jagged pathway through his hair. 'I have never been one for wearing my heart on my sleeve,' he said. 'I am not going to change now, not for anyone.'

'Then God help us,' she said, 'for I can't see this relationship lasting more than a month or two at most.'

He clenched his hands into fists. 'Why do you have to push and push and push?' he asked. 'Why can't you just leave the past where it belongs? We both screwed up. I get that, OK? I am not blaming you. Not any more.'

'Y-you're not?' Her voice came out as a whisper.

He sighed and rubbed his hand over his face. 'No,' he finally said, holding out an arm for her. 'Come here.'

Bronte went.

CHAPTER TWELVE

LUCA wrapped his arms around her, holding her close to him and, burying his face in her hair, he pressed a kiss to the top of her head.

It seemed a decade before he spoke and, when he did, his voice sounded scratchy and uneven. 'I'm sorry you had to find out like that,' he said. 'I wanted to spare you the gory details. I like to pretend it didn't happen.'

Bronte couldn't stop the flow of tears. 'Oh, Luca, don't you see that I need to know everything because that's the only way we can get our relationship to work?'

He brushed at her tears with his thumbs. 'I didn't want to make you feel sorry for me. I couldn't bear to be pitied. How could I be sure you were back with me because you wanted to be or because you felt sorry for me?'

She swallowed a knot of dread. 'Your grand-father said—'

'He was right,' Luca said grimly. 'I had an unexpected complication. I had a bleed which put me into a coma for three weeks. No one knew how I would be when I woke up, even if I *would* wake up. Just like what had happened to my father. I couldn't bear ending up like that, sitting drooling vacantly in a chair with no recognition of all the people who most loved me. How could I do that to my family? How could I do that to you?'

Bronte could finally see now why he had acted as he had. He had been so concerned for her that he had put his own hopes and dreams aside to set her free in case something went horribly wrong. Instead of seeing what he did as selfish and ruthless, she now saw it for what it was: the most honourable, selfless thing anyone could do for someone they loved. 'That's why you let me go the way you did, wasn't it?' she asked. 'You wanted me to think you no longer had any feelings for me. It's why you never told me what you felt the whole time we were together. You

always were going to let me go because you
wanted me to be safe from a lifetime of caring
for you if it all went wrong because you knew
I would never turn my back on you.'

He met her gaze, his throat rising and falling
over a tight swallow. 'It was the hardest thing
I've ever had to do,' he said. 'I knew if I did
it in person I would not be able to walk away
from you. I was so close to telling you a couple
of times about my condition but I talked myself
out of it. I didn't want your pity. I didn't want to
tie you down out of obligation and duty.'

She choked over the words. 'I...I would have
stood by you, Luca, surely you know that?'

'That was the problem, *cara*,' he said. 'I knew
you would stand by me, no matter what, but I
couldn't allow you to do that. What if the worst
had happened? I could have become an invalid
or mentally disabled. It's happened before. The
brain can't survive long periods without oxygen.
Multiple seizures can cause irreparable damage.
I just couldn't risk ruining your life. You had
the world at your feet. You were so talented. I
was sure you would end up at the London Ballet

academy. I would have held you back. I had to let you go.'

Bronte put her arms tightly around his waist, her tears soaking the front of his shirt. 'I never stopped loving you, Luca,' she sobbed. 'I've been fooling myself for all this time that I hated you but really I didn't. I could never hate you.'

Luca breathed in the fragrance of her hair as he held her against him. 'I was hoping I hadn't totally destroyed what you felt for me,' he said in a gravelly voice. 'I had to wait until I was given the all-clear. I promised myself a full year without a single seizure and then I would contact you. It felt like a lifetime. I didn't realise that it *was* a lifetime: Ella's lifetime.'

Bronte looked up at him with glistening eyes. 'She loved you from the moment she met you, Luca. You don't have to worry about her not realising you weren't there for the first bit of her life. When she's old enough, we can explain. The important thing is that you're here now. You are her father. You have always been her father. I have never thought of you as anything else.'

He smiled a half smile. 'I love you, you do

realise that, don't you? I have loved you from the first time I met you. You are my heart, my reason for living. I love you so much it hurts.'

Her eyes watered all over again. 'I think it's just starting to dawn on me.'

He brushed a strand of her hair off her face in a tender gesture, his dark eyes meltingly soft as they meshed with hers. 'I fell in love with you the day we met in that London bookshop. Do you remember when you bumped into me and you dropped your handbag and it scattered its contents all over the floor?'

Bronte smiled. 'That's how you got my address, wasn't it? You checked my diary before you handed it to me.'

'What was a desperate man to do?' he asked with a grin. 'I wanted to see you again. I felt an instant attraction. I had never felt anything like that before. When our fingers met when I handed you your tub of lipgloss I felt as if I was being electrocuted. My fingers were still tingling hours later.'

'Mine were too,' she said, slipping her arms up around his neck.

He bent down and planted a soft, lingering kiss to her mouth. When he finally lifted his head Bronte was looking up at him dazedly. 'I can't believe this is happening,' she said. 'I used to dream of one day seeing you again. I never thought it would really happen.'

'I am sorry things worked out the way they did,' he said. 'But I am not sure I wouldn't do things the same way again. I loved you too much to wilfully destroy your life.'

'Did you tell *anyone* about your condition?' she asked.

'Not until it was over,' he said. 'I had left a letter with my lawyer in case of an emergency. The doctors had orders to contact him if things didn't go according to plan, which, of course, he then had to do when I slipped into a coma. My family, of course, were terribly upset, as you can imagine, my mother in particular. She had already lost one child and had never got over it, as you heard downstairs. Giorgio was very good about it but Nic was pretty cut up. But I think he's more or less forgiven me by now.'

Bronte caressed his face lovingly. 'I'm so

glad you told me, Luca. I was so worried about marrying you just for Ella's sake. It didn't seem right. I was frightened you might take her away from me, you know, fight for custody or something.'

A frown interrupted his features. 'I have seen the drama that my brother and sister-in-law are currently going through over their dog. Neither of them wants to compromise. I didn't want to put either of you through that. I was determined to make things work out. I just felt you needed a bit of time.'

She gave him a mock-reproachful look. 'And a little bit of pressure.'

'Well,' he said with a sheepish grin, 'a man's got to do what a man's got to do.'

She snuggled up even closer. 'Definitely,' she said on a sultry purr. 'Especially if you are serious about wanting to make a brother or sister for Ella.'

His eyes lit up. 'You mean you're ready to try for another baby?'

She smiled and wriggled against him suggestively. 'You bet I am. So how about you get on with it?'

Luca smiled and pulled down the shoestring straps of her nightgown. 'Just try and stop me, *cara*,' he said and pressed her back down on the bed, his mouth coming down on hers.

Two weeks later...

Bronte stood at the end of the aisle and looked down at Luca, standing waiting for her by the altar. The organ was playing, the congregation was smiling, the flowers and their heady scent filled the air with hope and happiness and love.

She caught her mother's eye and smiled. Ella chortled in Tina Bennett's arms and called out volubly, 'Mummy pretty, Mummy berry pretty.'

'Mummy is beautiful,' Luca said as Bronte came to stand beside him.

'Hi,' she said softly.

'Hi yourself,' he said, taking her hands in his, squeezing them gently. 'You're trembling.'

'I'm nervous.'

'Don't be, *tesore mio*,' he said. 'This is the beginning of our life together. Our life as a family.'

The priest began the poignant service and at the end there was barely a dry eye in the house. Bronte was enveloped by Luca's family as she and Luca came out of the church when it was over. Even Giorgio and Maya had seemed to put their enmity to one side so as not to spoil Luca and Bronte's special day.

Luca's mother mopped at her eyes and smiled as she pulled Bronte into a bone-crushing hug. Over the last couple of weeks she had softened towards Bronte and had spent many a happy day preparing for the wedding with her. Bronte felt that Giovanna's love for Ella more than made up for any ill feeling that had been there at their first meeting.

'Welcome to the family, Bronte,' Giovanna said. 'You have given my son so much joy. You have given me so much joy. I don't know how to thank you.'

'He's easy to love,' Bronte said, looking in

Luca's direction, her breath coming out in a heartfelt sigh of happiness. 'So very easy to love.'

Giovanna smiled with maternal pride. 'Yes, he is,' she said. 'I am so glad he found you again. I don't think he would have settled for anyone else, you know. Luca's father was the same, although the death of our daughter set him off course for a while, but he finally came back to me. He knew there would be no other woman who could love him like I loved him.'

Bronte felt her heart give a little jump of excitement as Luca came back and slipped his arm around her waist.

'What family secrets is my mother letting out of the bag?' he asked playfully.

'Your mother was telling me you are just like your father,' Bronte said, exchanging a conspiratorial look with the older woman.

Luca pressed a kiss to the tip of Bronte's upturned nose. 'Did she tell you that once a Sabbatini man falls in love it is for ever?' he asked.

'She didn't need to tell me that,' Bronte said on a blissful sigh as his protective arms enfolded her. 'That's something I already knew.'

0111 Rom LP

MILLS & BOON PUBLISH EIGHT LARGE PRINT TITLES A MONTH. THESE ARE THE EIGHT TITLES FOR FEBRUARY 2011.

————————— ❡ —————————

THE RELUCTANT SURRENDER
Penny Jordan

SHAMEFUL SECRET, SHOTGUN WEDDING
Sharon Kendrick

THE VIRGIN'S CHOICE
Jennie Lucas

SCANDAL: UNCLAIMED LOVE-CHILD
Melanie Milburne

ACCIDENTALLY PREGNANT!
Rebecca Winters

STAR-CROSSED SWEETHEARTS
Jackie Braun

A MIRACLE FOR HIS SECRET SON
Barbara Hannay

PROUD RANCHER, PRECIOUS BUNDLE
Donna Alward

MILLS & BOON PUBLISH EIGHT LARGE PRINT TITLES A MONTH. THESE ARE THE EIGHT TITLES FOR MARCH 2011.

ↂ

THE DUTIFUL WIFE
Penny Jordan

HIS CHRISTMAS VIRGIN
Carole Mortimer

PUBLIC MARRIAGE, PRIVATE SECRETS
Helen Bianchin

FORBIDDEN OR FOR BEDDING?
Julia James

CHRISTMAS WITH HER BOSS
Marion Lennox

FIREFIGHTER'S DOORSTEP BABY
Barbara McMahon

DADDY BY CHRISTMAS
Patricia Thayer

CHRISTMAS MAGIC ON THE MOUNTAIN
Melissa McClone

Discover Pure Reading Pleasure with

Visit the Mills & Boon website for all the latest in romance

 Buy all the latest releases, backlist and eBooks

Find out more about our authors and their books

Join our community and chat to authors and other readers

Free online reads from your favourite authors

Win with our fantastic online competitions

Sign up for our free monthly eNewsletter

Tell us what you think by signing up to our reader panel

Rate and review books with our star system

www.millsandboon.co.uk

 Follow us at twitter.com/millsandboonuk

Become a fan at facebook.com/romancehq

75